Jonathan Corncob

Barabba —
    This caught my
fancy for some reason,
and it seemed to
be the perfect 45th
birthday book —
                M.

August 6, 1979

DULCE EST DESIPERE IN LOCO.

The
Adventures
OF
JONATHAN CORNCOB

𝕷𝖔𝖞𝖆𝖑 𝕬𝖒𝖊𝖗𝖎𝖈𝖆𝖓 𝕽𝖊𝖋𝖚𝖌𝖊𝖊.

——

Written by Himself

LONDON
PRINTED FOR THE AUTHOR, 1787
AND NOW NEWLY REPRINTED BY
DAVID R. GODINE · *Publisher*
BOSTON

First published in 1976 by
DAVID R. GODINE, *Publisher*
306 Dartmouth Street
Boston, Massachusetts

Copyright © 1976 by David R. Godine
Illustrations copyright © 1976 by Mark Livingston
ISBN 0-87923-184-X
LCC 75-43348

Printed in the United States of America

ADVENTURES

OF

JONATHAN CORNCOB,

LOYAL AMERICAN REFUGEE.

WRITTEN BY HIMSELF.

DULCE EST DESIPERE IN LOCO.

LONDON:

PRINTED FOR THE AUTHOR;

AND SOLD BY G. G. J. AND G. ROBINSON,
PATERNOSTER-ROW; AND R. FAULDER,
NEW BOND-STREET.

MDCCLXXXVII.

SPIRIT OF CONTRADICTION

TWO

SPIRIT OF '76 ANGELS

BUCKRAM

ONE AND

SPIRIT OF CONTENTION

M. Livingston Delt

Foreword

FORGOTTEN books are usually forgotten because they deserve to be—which does not, however, keep a great many of them from being reprinted. Obscure works from the American past slide back into print with especial frequency.

Some are resurrected because they belong to literary history. This one was an influence on Cooper, that one was the first picaresque novel published west of the Appalachians, and so on. Others reappear because they contribute to social history. Here is an account of bundling by an author who personally bundled as a young man in Hartford during the French and Indian wars; here is an artless view of George Washington before he vanished into the mantle of greatness; here is evidence that hominy grits were being eaten in western Maryland in 1803.

A few, a very few, books are reprinted because they still make good reading. *The Adventures of Jonathan Corncob* is one of this small number. It was a lively book when it was first published in 1787, and it makes, if anything, even livelier reading now. The hero is a Massachusetts farm boy who got mixed up in the American Revolution as a result of making a girl on the next farm pregnant. Given the choice of marrying Miss Desire Slawbunk or paying a fifty-pound fine, he runs away to Boston. (It's a quick trip, because he gets a ride most of the way on the back of a passing moose.)

Soon he is serving on an American privateer. Soon after that on a British man-o'-war. And presently he winds up in New York City, making cattle raids into New Jersey with a group of Loyalists and personal raids on a New York society girl named Dinah Donewell. Dinah is the granddaughter of the former Presbyterian minister of New York (the whole city was one parish until 1768)[1] and a young woman of breeding and education.

After recovering from the six or eight kinds of venereal disease she gives him, he hurries off to further adventures—with a more common Rhode Island girl named Dolly, with slaves and slave-owners in the Barbadoes, with a Royal Navy officer who is one of the few combatants in the American Revolution even more cowardly than Jonathan himself. When the book rather abruptly ends, he is back in New York. He is reunited with Desire Slawbunk, now the widow of a British company commander and more amorous than ever. He is in several kinds of trouble, as usual.

As this summary suggests, the book does not paint a reverent or a heroic picture of the Revolution. On the contrary, it is to that war pretty much what Joseph Heller's *Catch-22* is to the Second World War. *Jonathan Corncob* is eighteenth-century black humor, rich in absurdity. Captain Quid of the British Navy who surrenders to the American privateer *Picaroon* without firing a shot—and who is exonerated by a board of brother captains, while his gunnery officer, who wanted to fight, is sentenced to three months in prison for impudence—Captain Quid is an absurd figure. So is Captain O'Sneak of the British Army, a man still more prudent than Quid. So is Lieutenant Hastendudenrot of His Majesty's Hessian troops, who spends most of the war relieving American civilians of their valuables. 'If you vas one frynd to the Koning,' he points out to any prosperous American he meets, 'you vas gif me your vatch; if you vas one repell, by Got I take it.'

The Americans, beginning with Jonathan himself, are equally lacking in heroics. Their very names make that clear. 'Corncob' speaks for itself, while 'Jonathan' is a name that eighteenth-century Englishmen delighted to use to epitomize American rusticity. When the British under General Gage evacuated their position on Bunker Hill in 1775, they left a message for the advancing Americans, written in letters of hay. 'Welcome, Brother Jonathan,' it said.[2] As late as 1838, an Englishwoman visiting New

York noted with interest that the locals found the name Jonathan "highly offensive," at least from English lips.[3]

Every other male American in the book gets an offensive name, too—or at least an absurdly Biblical one. Real New Englanders at the time mostly had names like John, as in John Adams, and Ethan, as in Ethan Allen. Biblical but pronounceable. Jonathan's father is Mr. Habakkuk Corncob; Desire is the daughter of old Benaniah Slawbunk. Jonathan's many brothers include Zedekias, Hannaniah, Melchisedeck, and little Jeptha. His two sisters, pretty girls but not at all virginal, have absurd names in another style. They are the Misses Supply Corncob and Increase Corncob. The book is as disrespectful to sturdy Americans as it is to the effete English.

But the author's effrontery goes beyond that. He not only mocks both sides in the Great Patriotic War, he contrives to be racist, sexist, anti-religious, and wonderfully obscene in the process. He sticks bawdy details in the obscurest places. Even Jonathan's father's farm in Massachusetts, ostensibly bearing one of those Indian names so funny to English ears, like Pocasset and Wequetequock, has an obscene echo. Old Mr. Corncob lives at Squatcock Farm. As for his girl friend, Miss Desire Slawbunk, her last name is a slight corruption of a word once common in New York and New Jersey. The early Dutch settlers used to recline on what they called a *slaap bancke,* or sleeping bench. This phrase came into colonial American speech as 'slawbank,' still meaning something you lie down on. Its applicability to Desire is increasingly obvious as one reads the book.[4]

All this was clearly apparent to the original readers in 1787. 'Harkee, Mr. Jonathan Corncob!' one of the earliest reviews began.[5] 'Leave your indecorums, and preserve your genuine humor, unpolluted by improper language.' Another reviewer, correctly spotting a resemblance to Smollett (though Sterne was the author's conscious model), wrote, 'It would have been well if the author had been as attentive to Smollett's decency, for Jonathan Corncob abounds so much in that broad humour, nearly bordering on obscenity, that we can by no means recommend his adventures to the perusal of our *female* readers.' Smollett's decency, indeed! The more usual view of Smollett was that he sadly lacked it.

This same reviewer, in the *General Magazine and Impartial Review,* concluded by expressing the hope that in future books the author of *Jonathan Corncob* would pay 'some attention to common decency, and some respect to the Christian religion.'[6] Others didn't even bother to hope. The *Gentleman's Magazine,* for example, dismissed the book and author in one sentence as beyond the pale.[7]

One thing none of the reviewers did was to

identify the author. He never has been identi-
fied. One or two reviewers did assume that he
was what he claimed to be—a banished American Loyalist, living in Europe. This was not a
wholly unreasonable assumption, since there
were a lot of banished Loyalists. Jonathan's
home state of Massachusetts alone sent some 310
of its citizens into exile. Many of them went to
England, and some of them whiled away their
time by writing. From the whole United States
there were something over six hundred Loyal
American Refugees drawing pensions from the
British government in 1783,[8] and an unknown
further number living on their own resources.
Taking for granted that the author of *Jonathan
Corncob* was one of these, the *Monthly Review*
criticized him for fouling his own nest by making such sport of American manners.

It is extremely improbable, however, that the
author was an American. The evidence of the
book suggests that he was much more likely a
Royal Navy officer who had served a long time
in America, and perhaps even been a prisoner
of war. Few people indeed have weighed the
evidence, because *Jonathan Corncob* is almost
totally unknown in America (there are fewer
than a dozen copies in the country), and long
since forgotten in England. At least one person
besides myself has considered the question,
though—the late R. W. G. Vail, for many years
director of the New York Historical Society,

and a devotee of Jonathan Corncob. Dr. Vail's conclusion is the same as mine. The author was probably a British naval officer.[9]

There are several pieces of evidence. One is simply the author's very great familiarity with nautical language in general, and Royal Navy customs in particular. Another is the special venom he reserves for the corrupt bureaucratic practices of the Admiralty—he keeps his mocking *Catch-22* tone, but here, and here alone, a genuine indignation peeps through. A third, which proves nothing about his being a naval officer but suggests his Englishness, is the occasional appearance of words not in the American vocabulary. The author had a pretty good ear for American speech, and he reproduces the dialogue of New England courtship quite funnily. But in ordinary narrative he sometimes uses words that an eighteenth-century American would not have been likely to.

Early in the book, for example, he has Jonathan going home dead drunk from Hull's Tavern in New York. This was a real place and a center of Loyalist activity. Jonathan is reeling up Broadway when, as he says, 'I stumbled over something [it soon turns out to be an equally drunk British sentinel] and fell into the kennel.' Kennel? Someone is keeping his dogs in the middle of Broadway? Not at all. Kennel in this sense is a variant of 'channel'—and it was the open ditch running down the center of Broadway that poor Jonathan fell into. In those days the street was only paved ten feet out from each side, and the rest was dirt, with a drain in the middle. In England such a drain was called a kennel. In America it was almost always called a sewer. ('Kennel' in its sewer sense does appear in early American dictionaries—but chiefly because early American dictionaries are all pirated from still earlier English dictionaries. The first one genuinely edited in this country didn't appear until 1806. When the drain was actually dug down Broadway, the City Council called it 'the Common sewer.')

There is also one argument against the author's being a Royal Navy officer. Most eighteenth-century naval officers were not particularly well educated, as a consequence of having gone to sea at age twelve or thirteen. But the author of *Jonathan Corncob* is a person of some learning. He has read Horace and Scipio, and quotes them both. When he wants a funny sex quotation, he turns to *King Lear*. When he wants a barb to throw at the New Testament, he adapts it from one of Falstaff's lines in *Henry IV, Part One*.[10] He has studied Newton's physics and Bernardin de St. Pierre's philosophy. There *were* educated British sailors who served in the Revolution, though. Commodore William Hotham, senior officer in New York in the late 1770s, had been to Westminster School and then the Royal Naval Academy. Admiral Howe, who succeeded him, spent five years at Eton before joining the Navy at the comparatively advanced age of fifteen and a half. The author's classical learning does not rule out the possibility of his having been a lieutenant or a purser on a British ship. What it does rule out is the possibility of his having been, like his hero, the son of an illiterate Yankee farmer.

Whoever wrote the book, it is a considerable addition to eighteenth-century literature. As I have already claimed, it is one of the tiny handful of early books about America that remains a pleasure to read. But it also has some historical importance. The book generally recognized as the first American novel is William Hill Brown's *The Power of Sympathy,* which came out in 1789, two years after *Jonathan Corncob.* There are earlier candidates, of varying implausibility, going back as far as Charlotte Lennox's *The Female Quixote,* 1752. Some of these 'novels' are thirty or forty pages long. Even counting them, the whole number is small. The total number of American novels published before 1820 is about a hundred, not many more than come out in any given week at the moment. Granted that *Jonathan Corncob* is probably not an American novel, but an English novel about America, it still represents a notable addition to this small company.

Or again, the total number of early novels, English or American, that in any way use the

American Revolution for background is well under a hundred. The number written from the American point of view is five. *Jonathan Corncob* is one of these five, and by far the best of them. There is a profound rightness in the book's having its first American edition—and second edition of any sort—during the two hundredth anniversary of that war.

In editing it, I have obviously followed the text of the London edition of 1787, since that is the only one there is. The original author put one footnote in the book—to identify that exotic American animal the skunk for English readers. With his for a precedent, I have sparingly added others. The Latin tag on the title page I will annotate right now. It is from Horace, and means, 'It is sweet to raise hell.' And though this is not intended as a scholarly edition, I have put a single page of references at the back. They are chiefly to identify sources used in this foreword.

In the last sentence of the book, the author half-promises to write a sequel, carrying Jonathan through the rest of the Revolution and into exile. I like to imagine that had he done so, he would have taken Desire Slawbunk Seeclear to England with Jonathan, and perhaps even to a good London dentist, so that her kisses would have been still more exciting than a remarkably large number of people in and out of the British army found them. But the sequel never appeared. The loss to American literature is a real one.

It only remains to yield the stage to Jonathan himself. I heartily recommend his adventures to the perusal of female and all other readers.

NOEL PERRIN
Hanover, New Hampshire
July 4, 1976

References

[1] *one parish until 1768:* Thomas E. V. Smith, *New York City in 1789.* N.Y.: 1889, p. 147.

[2] *Welcome, Brother Jonathan:* James T. Adams, ed., *Dictionary of American History*, N.Y.: 1940, III, 181.

[3] *As late as 1838: American Life,* by Mrs. Felton, London: 1842, p. 45. (1st ed., Hull: 1838.)

Note: 'Jonathan' and 'the Jonathans' were also terms used as nicknames for the American rebel army, much as 'Green' and 'the Big Green' are currently used for the Dartmouth football team.

   The *Royal Gazette* for October 8, 1778, for example, describes a battle between 'Jonathan' and the British for possession of Fairfield, Conn. On May 27, 1780, the same paper reported a skirmish won by 'Colonel Delancey with a party of his Loyal Refugees,' in which 'the Jonathans' lost eight killed and 34 captured. (Albert Matthews, 'Brother Jonathan,'

References
Colonial Society of Massachusetts Publications, Vol. VII, 1905, pp. 107-108.)

[4] *slawbank*: Mary Helen Dohan, *Our Own Words*, Baltimore: 1975. p. 129. See also Mitford Mathews, ed., *A Dictionary of Americanisms on Historical Principles*, Chicago: 1951, p. 1563.

[5] *Harkee!*: *Critical Review*, Feb., 1788, p. 150.

[6] *General Magazine:* Jan., 1788, p. 35.

[7] *Gentleman's Magazine:* Dec., 1787, p. 1095.

Note: The book was also reviewed in *The European Magazine*, Dec., 1787, p. 466, and *The Monthly Review*, Dec., 1787, p. 495. There were no American reviews. American book reviewing barely existed before 1800. *310 of its citizens:* George A. Ward, ed., *Letters and Journals of Samuel Curwen*, Boston: 1864, p. 24.

[8] *over six hundred:* Lorenzo Sabine, *The American Loyalists*, Boston: 1847, p. 70.

[9] *R. W. G. Vail:* See his '*Adventures of Jonathan Corncob, Loyal American Refugee:* A Commentary,' *Papers of the American Bibliographical Society*, Vol. 50, 2nd Quarter, 1956, p. 106.

[10] *Falstaff's lines:* Act II, Scene iv, 11. 174f.

The
Adventures
OF
JONATHAN CORNCOB

Contents

CHAPTER 1

PAGE

An Introduction   1

CHAPTER 2

*A short account of Jonathan's birth,
parentage, and education, and of the
ill consequences of an American
amusement called Bundling.*   5

CHAPTER 3

*Jonathan loses himself in a wood, and
is almost starved, when Providence
furnishes him a steed and hot dinner.
Arrives at Boston. A true technical
discipline of the royal navy.*   14

CHAPTER 4

*Jonathan is put in prison at Boston;
makes his escape on board an English*

Contents

PAGE

*ship, where he has a sample of the
discipline of the royal navy.*   20

Chapter 5

*Jonathan takes lodgings at New-York.
His amours with his landlady's niece;
and the bad consequences that follow.*   25

Chapter 6

*Jonathan has the good fortune to
escape with life from a most desperate
action, and the hands of two surgeons.*   32

Chapter 7

*A military execution; with the
character of Capt. Furnace of the
navy.*   39

Chapter 8

*Conversation between Captain
Furnace; Captain O'Sneak, a
half-pay captain of the army;
and the lieutenant of the ship.*   47

Chapter 9

*Jonathan meets with a disappointment
in love at Rhode Island; returns to*

[xxiv]

Contents

PAGE

New-York; meets unexpectedly with
an old acquaintance.   51

CHAPTER 10

Desire Slawbunk's narrative, and
subsequent conversation.   57

CHAPTER 11

The misfortunes of Mr. Habakkuk
Corncob. An American hunt.—
Jonathan quarrels with Captain
Seeclear.   61

CHAPTER 12

Jonathan goes to Barbadoes, and is
highly satisfied with that island.   67

CHAPTER 13

The West-Indian way of white-
washing, or rather the true way of
washing the blachamoor white.
Jonathan begins to lose his good
opinion of Barbadoes.   72

CHAPTER 14

A hurricane at Barbadoes, and an
account of the damage caused by it.   80

Contents

CHAPTER 15

Jonathan returns to New-York, where he is appointed purser of an armed brigantine.—Meets at sea with the Picaroon American privateer. The captain of Jonathan's brig obliged to strike, the commander of the Picaroon being one of the most obstinate fellows upon record.　　85

CHAPTER 16

Jonathan's sad reflections in gaol: meets with an alarm, which terminates agreeably.　　93

CHAPTER 17

Mrs. Seeclear's narrative.—Jonathan in a great danger experiences the efficacy of prayers.　　97

CHAPTER 18

Jonathan embarks on board a cartel-ship bound to New-York.—The gallant behaviour of Captain Quid, in the battle—he would have fought with the Picaroon, but for untoward circumstances.—Proceedings of a naval court-martial.　　108

Contents

CHAPTER 19

In which it is proved to the satisfaction of the most captious, that the most advantageous kind of study is novel reading.   116

Chapter 1

An Introduction

T HE MORNING was cold, gloomy, and foggy; in short it was one of those mornings so common in the happy island of Great Britain: the teeth of my lower jaw were in dispute with those above, my feet were frozen, and my nose was blue; all the horses on the western road had taken cold, were much troubled with a running at the nose, and incapable of going their usual pace, so that the diligence merited its name less than ever.

'Sir,' said an elderly gentleman in the other corner of the carriage, 'I beg your pardon for the question I am going to ask, but pray what may your age be?'

'Four and twenty,' answered I—'I did not think you older,' replied the gentleman, 'and was surprised to see you already bald. As I flatter myself that I am something of a physiognomist, I am convinced that the few years you have existed, have been marked by some extraordinary incidents, that have caused so early a loss of your toupet.'

'Your penetration, Sir,' said I, 'has not deceived you: I lost part of my hair in a sickness at New York; part was taken from me by the sea scurvy in the West Indies; I was deprived of part of what remained by a fright—,'

'By a fright?' said the gentleman, interrupting me—

'Yes, Sir,' said I, 'I walked in a fright, and my hair stood on end so obstinately afterwards, that I lost a great deal in reducing it to its former situation. The remaining part was blown away in a hurricane at Barbadoes.'

'Upon my word,' said the gentleman, 'this is a little extraordinary, and I am inclined to believe that your history must be highly amusing. If it is not taking too great a liberty, allow me to request a recital of it. We are still at a great distance from Salisbury; the horses have the glanders, and get on but slowly; the face of the country is dreary; and a narrative of your adventures will divert our attention from the cold.'

'I would comply with your request,' answered I, 'but really I have no talents for story-telling.'

'You are too modest,' replied my gentleman, 'I am sure you tell a story admirably, for I have not, since the death of my friend Sterne, seen a quainter phiz.'

'You are very obliging,' said I, 'and put it out of my power to refuse you any thing.'

I told my story: the gentleman laughed; said it was *strange, 'twas passing strange; 'twas pitiful, 'twas wondrous pitiful.* 'Were I you,' said he, 'I would write my history.'

At this time, I had money in my purse, and had little inclination for any kind of writing, except the fabrication of a few false signatures, that were necessary to enable me, as purser, to settle my accounts with the Navy Board. But now, banished from England by virtue of a writ taken out against me by a hard-hearted tailor; living on half the pay of a purser in ordinary, being obliged to give the other half to a reduced midshipman who does the duty as my deputy; under the necessity of passing my time in a garret in French Flanders, my nankeen breeches being worn out in the feat; dunned by the baker for bread to the amount of forty-four livres, and by the *traiteur* for a *fricandeau** of thirty sous, with which I indulged myself on Easter Sunday; I shall at least amuse myself by taking my fellow traveller's advice. I do not know whether I shall amuse anybody else: my quaint phiz will be wanting, and in that perhaps lay the principal merit of my tale—However as histories of prime ministers and pickpockets are often well received by the public, it is a strong presumption that the memoirs of a purser may succeed. It is besides out of my power to revisit England, for the purpose of representing my claims to the commissioners for the relief of distressed loyalists; but as my adventures may fall into their hands, they may perhaps attend to my many losses, independent of that of my toupet, which is of more consequences than may be imagined. I paid my addresses to a little

*Inn-keeper for a veal stew.

[3]

girl with a fortune of four thousand pounds. Every thing was agreed on. I had the mother's consent; I thought I had touched the daughter's heart, and pleased myself with the hope of soon touching her money, when my little inamorata, mounting one day on a chair, to give a lump of sugar to her canary bird, discovered the bareness of my scalp, took the first opportunity to quarrel with me, called me bald-pate, and shewed me the door.

Chapter 2

*A short account of Jonathan's birth,
parentage and education, and of
the ill consequences of an American
amusement called Bundling.*

SOME GREAT men have been suckled in a wood,
as was the immortal founder of Rome, and
others in a stable; but as I was neither destined for
the founder of an empire, nor of a religion, I
opened my eyes on this wicked world in as snug a
farm-house as any in Massachusetts-Bay. My honoured mother, Mrs. Charity Corncob, was an excellent woman: she bred like a rabbit; scolded all day
like a cat in love; and snored all night as loud as
the foreman of a jury on a tedious trial. During her
pregnancy, she dreamed that she was brought to
bed of a screech owl, and went to consult an old
woman in the neighbourhood who passed for a
witch. The old woman assured her that her dream
was an unlucky prognostic, and told her that if I
was not cut off in my youth, I should certainly die
at a more advanced age, either by some unforeseen
accident, or of some violent disease. My poor

mother burst into tears, and asked her if there was
no way of averting so cruel a destiny. The old
woman answered in the negative, and Mrs. Corncob returned home much distressed at what she
had heard. No sooner was I born than I began to
cry, and this circumstance tended not a little to
fortify my mother's faith in the prediction of the
ancient sybil.

'Poor dear boy,' said Mrs. Corncob, sighing, 'Oh!
that ever I should be doomed to be the mother of
so unlucky a child. However, one comfort is, that
he cannot be drowned while he carries about him
the caul that covered his face when he was born.'

But when I was a year and a half old, and she saw
me frequently fall and pull the chairs upon my
back, she had no longer any doubt of the fatal
prophecy. Wretched as she was made by these
gloomy omens, she did not communicate her fears
to my honoured father, Mr. Habakkuk Corncob,
as she was apprehensive of hurting his health, already in a weakly state, for he had been troubled
with the green sickness ever since a disappointment
in love, he met with at the age of two and twenty.

Mr. Habakkuk Corncob was a rigid Presbyterian;
he considered any man who played at cards as
irrevocably d--n'd, as well as any one who walked
out on a Sunday. He employed every part of that
day, that was not spent at the meeting-house, in
reading the book of Leviticus, for the instruction of
his family, and thought himself peculiarly indul-
gent, when, by way of amusement, he favoured us
with the history of Shadrach, Meshach, and Abed-
nego, or a few pages of the *Pilgrim's Progress.*

These were the only two books he considered as worthy his attention, except indeed that kind of almanack in which the different parts of the body are placed opposite the days of the month. This almanack was his oracle, and directed all his operations: he never cut his nails, but on the day marked Hands, so that by the time the month came round, his claws were as long as those of a mandarin. The only day on which he profited by the privileges of a husband, was that indicated by Secrets, and this perhaps was the reason why my mother, Mrs. Charity Corncob, poor woman, sometimes advised him to take an almanack of another kind.

Though my father's state of health was infirm, it was much superior to that of my aunt, Lord have mercy on her soul! She had been thirty years troubled with an asthma, which unluckily turned to a consumption, just when she had hopes of getting rid of it. Whether it was owing to her ill health, or natural disposition, I know not, but she was a plague to every body in the house, from Mr. Habakkuk my father, to our black cur dog.

One day, after quarrelling with my father and mother, and boxing the ears of every child in the house, finding herself left without any person to scold, she jumped up, and kicked the cat round the room. The cat escaped out of the window, and my poor aunt was obliged to take up the poker, and poke the fire out. She might perhaps have lived somewhat longer, if she had not fallen into a dispute with my father about her age. My father asserted strenuously that she was fifty-two years old; my aunt said she was only forty-eight.

Forty-eight!

The Triumph of AUNT BATHSHEBA

M. Livingston Invt & Delt :: 1976

'Fifty-two,' said my father.

'Forty-eight,' said my aunt.

'Fifty-two,' said my father again.

At length my aunt finding herself out of breath, mustered up all her strength, with a determination of having the *last word,* called out forty-eight, and expired. At this time I was only seven years old, and when I heard the news, I came jumping and laughing into the room, 'Old Bathsheba is dead,' said I, '*ha! ha! ha!*'

My mother, who was making a violent lamentation, ran up to me, and, letting down my breeches, laid me across her knee, and flogged me till I joined my tears to those of the rest of the family; though I did not very well understand why I was obliged to cry at the death of a person, whom every body in the house had wished dead a thousand times a day.—All the neighbors crowded to our house to condole with us, and as they unanimously said my aunt was in heaven, the whole family was soon consoled, and the next day we were all as merry as ever.

Providence had certainly ordained that my aunt Bathsheba should be as great a plague to us when dead as she was when living. A few days after she was buried, my father took his gun down from the hooks over the chimney, with the intention of shooting a few squirrels for our supper. About half an hour after, he rushed pale and breathless into the room, threw himself into a chair, and called for a glass of New-England rum. My mother, and the rest of us, alarmed at his situation, asked all together what was the matter. As soon as he recovered

[9]

a little from his fright, he told us, that he had seen the spirit of Bathsheba. My mother started; my four brothers, my two sisters and myself, all opened our mouths.

'Yes,' continued he, 'I have seen the spirit of Bathsheba; I am sure of it. I was scarcely in the wood before I met with a large black wild turkey; I immediately cocked my gun, put it to my shoulder, and was going to *blaze away*, when the turkey called out *forty-eight*, as plain as it could speak, and ran off towards the churchyard. I swear it could be nobody but Bathsheba, for it had just her waddling way of walking.'

My father and mother were so afraid of a visit from the wild turkey, that for a long time after they kept a light all night in their bed-room, which, as far as it related to the bed-room, had the desired effect; but did not prevent my mother from seeing Bathsheba in the dairy. Mrs. Corncob was found there in a swoon by my eldest sister, and as soon as she recovered her speech, told us that she had seen Bathsheba, in the shape of a black cat, stealing cream.

'What made me sure of it,' said my mother, 'was her having only one eye like my poor dear cousin, and her coming to the dairy exactly at the time Bathsheba used to drink her bowl of milk in the afternoon.' In a short time there was not one of us that had not seen our aunt in the shape of something black, and we no longer dared to go to bed till we had visited every room in the house, and made a very scrupulous search after my aunt Bathsheba.

My father, who had never learned to write, often

regretted that he was not scholar enough to lay Bathsheba's ghost, and determined that my education should not be neglected, especially as he destined me to superintend his shop, or as it is called in New-England, his *store,* for he was not only farmer, but merchant, and sold butter, cheese, spike-nails, rye meal, shuttlecocks, New-England rum, hartshorn shavings, broad cloth, gunpowder, and yellow basilicon. Besides the inferior parts of education, such as reading, writing, and arithmetick, I studied Latin, and at the end of seven years made very tolerable nonsense verses. I was considered, in Massachusetts-Bay, as a prodigy of learning, and was not less distinguished for my address in all the fashionable exercises and amusements of that country. I excelled in walking in snow shoes, driving a sled, shooting squirrels, and bobbing for eels; but of all my amusements none had such charms for me as *bundling.*

I had already bundled with half the girls in the neighborhood, when my evil genius led me to pay a visit to Miss Desire Slawbunk, one evening when her father and mother were gone out. Miss Slawbunk was an American beauty; her complexion was a little dusky, her features regular, and she had a certain languor in her look that was not unpleasing. Unfortunately she preferred molasses to all other sauces: whether she ate pickled pork or kidney beans, she never failed to, call for molasses, and owing to this immoderate use of it, had lost six of her front teeth above, and six below.

'I swear now, Miss Desire,' said I, 'I am come to *tarry* a little with you.'

'I guess you *be* very welcome, Mr. Jonathan.'

'It is a *considerable of* a cold night.'

'Yes,' answered Desire, *'some cold.'*

This remark of the coldness of the weather made the lady observe, that her fire was by no means brilliant. After in vain arranging the green wood, she stooped down before the fire in a sitting posture, and began puffing with her apron. It would not do, and Miss Slawbunk, wishing to produce more wind, had recourse to her petticoats. The inexorable logs still refused to burn. Miss Slawbunk grew angry, and the undulations of her petticoats grew proportionately wider and more violent. It was then that, sitting in the chimney corner, my discoveries became every moment more interesting; every faint gleam of the languid fire presenting to my eyes a soft assemblage of light and shade, that vied with all the snow and forests of the continent. Without improving the fire, she had produced an equal effect: her exertions had warmed herself, and what I had seen had changed my aguish shivering to a high fever. Though I had not come with any such intention, I could not help proposing to bundle. Miss Slawbunk consented, smiling very kindly, but, as you will suppose, without shewing her teeth.

We undressed according to the rules of bundling, scrupulously reserving the breeches and underpetticoat. Soon after we were in bed, my hand happening to touch Desire, she started from me.

'Miss Slawbunk,' said I, 'it seems to me that you be *considerable* ticklish.'

Miss Slawbunk denied it.

To prove my assertion, I began to tickle her

under the fifth rib. She tickled me in her turn, and by degrees we carried the pleasantry so far, that without being aware of the consequences, we exceeded all the bounds of bundling. Heaven only can tell what became of the petticoat during the night, but in the morning we found it kicked out of the foot of the bed. A few months after, it grew too short for Miss Slawbunk; a committee was assembled, and I was sentenced, for this breach of the laws of bundling, to marry the lady, or pay a fine of 50£ currency.

Not being inclined to comply with the first proposal, and being unable to pay the fine, I sold to some British officers, prisoners on parole in the neighborhood, a quantity of my father's New-England spirits, and exchanged with them all the brown paper-money of the Congress I could collect, for twenty hard dollars, which, as they were a rarity in that country, I secured in the waistband of my breeches, and with this small fortune determined to set off for New-York, then in the possession of the British troops.

Chapter 3

*Jonathan loses himself in a wood, and
is almost starved, when Providence
furnishes him a steed and hot dinner.
Arrives at Boston. A true technical
description of a sea-fight.*

I SET OFF before the dawn of day, and took my
road along the bypaths and through the woods,
dreading the sight of anybody I knew as much as a
half-pay officer does that of a creditor. This precaution had nearly been fatal to me, for after two days'
march I found myself in a forest that seemed to
have no end. I wandered about two whole days,
trying to find something eatable, but nothing could
I see, except blue-tailed jays, that, chattering and
hopping from branch to branch, seemed to make a
game of me. I was just bestowing a million of
maledictions on Miss Slawbunk's under-petticoat,
when, between two large trees that formed a small
opening, I observed the track of deer, and soon
after saw several pass along at full gallop. I climbed
four or five feet up one of the trees, and presently
a long string of moose deer, as tall as *dray horses,*
came thundering by me. I wounded several with

my knife as they passed, and, hoping some of them might fall, jumped off to follow them, when one that was behind turning short round the tree, I found myself astride on his back. My steed, who doubtless had the best wind of any moose deer in America, kept going all night like a devil, and made such abominable bounds, that, though I am a pretty good horseman, I must confess I have passed my time more agreeably. An hour after day-break I reached the outskirts of the wood, and having no longer occasion for my moose deer as a saddle-horse, and hunger pressing me, I began to butcher him, giving him stab after stab about the neck and head. He kicked and plunged so furiously that I lost a stirrup, and was nearly dismounted; however, I held myself on by his ears, and at last down he came like a bullock. I cut off a rump steak, and after saying a short grace, devoured it hot, and found it excellent.

The place where I alighted so hastily was not far from the road to Boston, to which town I determined to proceed, for the purpose of recruiting my health, that had suffered a great deal from long fasting and fatigue. On my arrival I found a great crowd assembled in the street. Curious to know the occasion of it, I thrust my nose into the midst of the populace, and saw a naked man lying on the pavement, while several others poured hot tar upon him. Soon after a large quantity of feathers was brought, in which he was rolled, and after the application of some long quills to his tail, this non-descript animal was suffered to rise.

I inquired what was the reason of this punishment, and was told that it was inflicted in consequence of the culprit's having fished in Boston harbour with a drag net, and caught a chest of tea. The tea had been thrown over-board from an English ship, by the pious Bostonians some years before, but as the double cover of wood and lead had preserved it from injury, the offender had sold it to his neighbours, contrary to law. He asserted in his defence, that he had not exacted the duty of three-pence per pound, but this excuse would not do, as it was six weeks since the Bostonians had tarred and feathered anybody.

Accompanied by the hooting populace he was driven out of the town, at the entrance of which, conducted by his ill-fortune, was a Micmac Indian, who was come eleven hundred miles on foot to sell a beaver's and two raccoons' skins. He no sooner saw our monster close to his nose, than staring with astonishment, he gave a howl like a flogged pointer, went to the right about, ran off like the wind, and, for any thing I know to the contrary, is running still.

Before I recovered my health, my small stock of money was nearly exhausted, and my scheme of proceeding to New-York became for the present impracticable. I therefore entered as a clerk in a privateer, that was on the point of sailing. After having been three days at sea, we fell in with an English vessel of nearly our own force, Cape Cod bearing W.N.W. 3/16 W. distant 25 leagues and a half. We kept our luff in hopes of gaining the wind, but not being able to fetch into the enemy's wake, we were obliged to pass under his lee, at

A CIVIC ENTERTAINMENT, AS
furnished by y̆ inhabitants of BOSTON

M.Livingston Delt.

three-fifths of a cable's length distance, and began the action at half past two P.M. We then shot ahead, and throwing the ship up in the wind across the enemy's forefoot, we raked him fore and aft with considerable success, but as his bow pointed for our chesttree* we were afraid of his running us aboard, and laid our head-sails aback, when the ship paid round off, and we engaged him, the main and fore course to the mast, for more than three glasses.

At four P.M. our captain turning round to me, had only time to say, 'I *snort* now, brother Jonathan, they blaaze away like daavils' when a cannon-ball broke his head, to my great astonishment. At this moment I believe we should have struck, if the English ship had not had a drum and fife upon deck playing Yankee Doodle. Our indignation at the insult kept up our courage, and we continued the action till five P.M. when the enemy hauled his wind: we should have pursued him, but unfortunately our mizzen-top-gallant stay-sail bow-line, and smoke-sail halyards were shot away, which it was necessary to knot and splice before we could renew the action. Our killed and wounded amounted to seven, including the captain in the number of the former, and among the latter our mizzen-mast.

Some of my readers may perhaps complain that I have been too prodigal of seamen's terms in my relation of the action; but I appeal to those masterpieces in this way, the letters of Admirals A. B. &c.,

---

*A wooden block to secure the lower corners of the mainsail. More picturesquely called the chess-tree and the cheese-tree. (All three terms derive from the French *chassis*.)

in spite of ill-natured people, who assert they had an interest in making them unintelligible.

After our rigging was repaired, we proceeded on our cruise, chasing several vessels without success, till on the banks of Newfoundland we met with a Dutchman, bound from Curassoa to Amsterdam. Our lieutenant, who commanded, had been, before the war, a cod fisherman in these latitudes, and as he had never been accustomed to return to port without catching something, he hit upon the expedient of hoisting English colours, and plundering the Hollander. We took about half his cargo, leaving him to make his complaint to the British minister, of this violation of the laws of nations, and returned to port, the stratagem of our lieutenant being universally applauded by his countrymen.

Chapter 4

Jonathan is put in prison at Boston;
makes his escape on board an
English ship, where he has a sample
of the discipline of the Royal Navy.

A DAY or two after I went to a shop to purchase
some trifling things for which I had occasion,
and found there an old gentleman, who was buying
a skein of thread. When he had received his purchase, he took out of his pocket a leathern bag drawn
up in the form of a purse, opened it, drew out of
it a black pocket-book, untied half a dozen knots,
undid as many turns of green binding, opened the
pocket-book with great caution and deliberation,
and at length produced a bill of the Congress for
six-pence. The money of the Congress had at this
time lost three-fourths of its original value.

He received in change a three-penny bill, and put
it into his pocket-book, which he tied up with as
much ceremony as he had opened it. While he was
employed in this operation he observed me take
out of my pocket some twenty- and thirty-dollar
bills, which I had received as my share of the plun-

der of the Dutchman, and which were rumpled up as if they had been waste-paper.

'I swear now,' said the old gentleman, 'but you seem to make very light of that money.'

'Why indeed,' answered I, tossing the bills up in the air, and catching them again in my hand, 'it must be confessed that this money is not very heavy.'

'I guess now,' replied the old gentleman, 'that you be a tory rogue, and it is such villains as you that depreciate the money of the state.' He then left the shop, to all appearance in great passion. I was not a little surprised, on leaving it soon after in my turn, to find myself taken into custody by six militiamen, with ragged coats and rusty muskets, who carried me before the Committee of Safety. My old friend, a tailor by trade and one of the committee, accused me of high treason, asserting, that I made a jest of the resources of the state. I alleged in my defence my love for my country, and my services in the action with the English ship: their honours, the Committee, were deaf to my reasoning, and ordered me to be taken to gaol.

After I had been there about two months, I heard that the Americans had been defeated by the King's troops, that the Bostonians were much out of spirits, and that to divert their attention from their misfortunes, as well as by way of revenge, they had determined to tar and feather me, together with a number of other state prisoners, on the following Thursday. This news induced us to endeavor to make our escape: we began by removing a large stone, and found the earth underneath very favourable for working a subterraneous passage, at which one half of us was employed, while the other half sung and danced, that the noise of the working party might not be overheard.

A passage was soon mined into the street, and we made a precipitate retreat through the town of Boston, on Wednesday night. At Hancock's wharf we fortunately found a very small schooner ready for sea, into which we jumped, hoisted the sails, and were under way in a moment. At the break of day we joined a British ship cruising in Boston bay, and were taken aboard it without difficulty. The captain was what is called in the navy a d––d smart officer: when any thing went wrong at the mast-head, he called out to the sailors, Aloft, oh! you lubbers; but left them to find out themselves the cause of their embarrassment. When in working the ship all had been declared ready on the fore-castle, and a rope afterwards proved foul, he told the lieutenant stationed there, through a speaking trumpet, that he lied; and when in windy weather the men in the maintop could not hear him, he flogged them all round. Happening one day to ob-serve a thick smoke issue from under the door of the boatswain's store-room, I ran upon deck, and addressing myself to the captain, 'Sir', said I, 'the boatswain's—'

'You d––d rascal,' said the captain, pushing me over to the other side of the deck, 'speak to the officer of the watch.'

I took my hat off to the lieutenant, 'Your honour, the boatswain's store—'

The lieutenant gave me a kick in the backside,

and said, if it was about stores I must go to the master. I went to the master, and said, 'Sir, the boatswain's store-room—'

The master, who was calculating the ship's course, only d——d me, and sent me to his mate. Luckily the mate heard me out, but, as I imagined the report would be made to the captain by the same gradations, and that his orders would descend by the same degrees, I concluded that His Majesty's good ship would be burned to the water's edge before the first bucket could be filled. No such thing. The mate no sooner heard that there was a fire in the boatswain's store-room, then he began to give orders himself. The captain and officers did the same; the sailors imitated their example; everybody commanded, nobody obeyed, and we were in a fair way to be roasted, to the great satisfaction of the pious Bostonians, if the master, a man of a cool head, had not placed a row of sentinels along the deck, to keep a passage open for the water, which soon overcame its rival element.

A few days after, the wind increased by degrees to a heavy gale, and all hands were ordered up to furl the top-sails. Two other Americans and myself, who had never been aloft, pleaded our inability to the lieutenant; he, by way of answer, sent for a boatswain's mate.

'Bear a hand,' said he, 'and lather these three fellows till they go aloft.' My two countrymen, after a few lashes, went up the shrouds; but as the ship rolled exceedingly, and as the wind was so high, that it was impossible for any thing but a monkey or a sailor to hold by the rigging, the poor fellows were blown overboard, and we lost sight of them in a moment. Nobody seemed to take much notice of their loss, except the lieutenant, who observed, that they sung out lustily for assistance. As I had obstinately refused to go aloft, I was tied up, and by the captain's order received a dozen lashes. I then supposed all was over, as I had heard that it was forbid to give more for a single fault; but the commander ordered me a second dozen for disobedience of orders, a third for neglect of duty, and a fourth for disrespect. He assured me that he would have given me twice as much, but that he had the goodness to consider me as young in the service. I thanked him for his lenity, but could not help complaining of the hardness of the alternative, which left no medium between being blown overboard, and having my back torn to pieces with nine lengths of knotted cord. An old sailor who was standing by me laughed, and told me it was a little sample of the discipline of the navy, and that when I had been flogged half a dozen times with the thief's cat,* I should think nothing of such a tickling.

*A cat-o'-nine-tails with more than the usual number of knots.

Chapter 5

Jonathan takes lodgings at New-York.
His amours with his landlady's niece,
and the bad consequences that follow.

AS SOON as I was landed at New-York, I associated myself with a party of Loyalists, who having been driven from their estates, plundered with great propriety all those in the vicinity. Their incursions were frequent in the Jerseys and Connecticut, and they seldom returned without bringing with them some few head of cattle prisoners. My employment among them consisted in keeping an account of the sale of the booty, as well as of the distribution of its produce, and I was scarcely ever engaged in any of their expeditions.

I lodged at New York, at the house of an old gentlewoman, who being reduced in her circumstances, was obliged to keep a chandler's-shop. As her father had been a Presbyterian parson, she had received a suitable education, and was a woman of considerable reading. Peculiarly well versed in the Old Testament, she was acquainted with all its personages, from Abishag the Shunamite, who lay with old David to keep his feet warm, to Bildad the Shuhite, who was a greater plague to Job than all his misfortunes. As I was always of a pious turn, I was exceedingly fond of her conversation, only I thought she made somewhat too free with respectable characters. She said Lot was a nasty old dog. King David stood pretty high in her good graces; she approved very much the abhorrence he showed of adultery, by the speedy means he used to divorce Bathsheba from her husband. She did not scruple to say that Solomon was *stark naught*: a man who was not satisfied with three hundred wives, all princesses too, but kept seven hundred mistresses, could have no conscience. When she was in a calculating humour, she lamented exceedingly the joyless life these ladies must have led, even supposing Solomon equal to a Turk and an Irishman together.

Her personal qualities were by no means answerable to her mental accomplishments. One eye pointed one way, the other another, and her nose a third. One corner of her mouth reached her temple, while the other end was behind her ear. It seemed as if her features were frightened at each other, and wished severally to make their escape. Her teeth had already done so, except two exactly in the center of that diagonal opening she called her mouth, and they, in shape and in colour, very nearly resembled a kitchen poker. She had a niece who lived with her, of the same religious turn as herself; but whose face had not any resemblance of her aunt's. She had a pretty little set of features perfectly charming. A little mouth that tempted you to be impertinent, and a little nose that op-

QVASI

AMOR VINCIT OMNIA

SHARP LOVE-PANGS, OR DINAH'S FIT

M. Livingston DELT

posed no obstacle to the completion of your desires. At the same time she looked as modest as a Lucrece, and had that kind of listless languor in her countenance, which I had remarked in my dear Desire Slawbunk's. However, Dinah Donewell, my landlady's niece, had not, like her, lost her teeth, as I experienced to my cost. Dinah, poor girl, was troubled with hysteric fits, and was attacked by them one evening when we were sitting together. I had recourse to the first remedy used by all young men on similar occasions. To give her room, I took her handkerchief from her neck, and loosened her stays. Heavens! what charms dazzled my eyes. The ecstasies of Columbus when he saw the land were not equal to my admiration of what I discovered. There, duly separated, lay two snowy twins, so firm, so elastic, so rebellious, that when touched they returned the blow. I thought the milky way between led on to heaven, unlike the madman Lear, who exclaimed.

Down to the waist they're angels; but devils all below:
There, there's the sulphurous pit.

The fair one's fits redoubled, and I recovered from my trance. I roared out to her, 'Dinah! Dinah! my dear Dinah!' I shook her; I sprinkled her face; I flapped the palms of her hands; I patted her back; I rubbed her temples; I tickled her nostrils; I pulled her ears; I opened her fingers; I pricked her under the nails; I almost suffocated her with burnt rags, feathers, and *eau de luce.** In

*Named after M. Luce, the inventor. A sort of cologne water with a lot of ammonia in it. Used in India to treat snake bites and in Europe as the most powerful of smelling salts.

short, I used all the customary gentle, well-imagined means to correct this disorder of the animal spirits, in vain. The lady, as is usual, grew ten times worse, and while I held her hands, bit my arm so heartily that she made her teeth meet. Although I did not know but a dose of human flesh might be a specific in this malady, I did not fail, according to the expression of the sea-lieutenant, to *sing* out lustily. My cries brought Mrs. Donewell to my assistance, who called me noodle, and desired me to leave the cure to her. Wetting a napkin in cold water, she knelt down before her niece, and introducing it between her feet, applied it the *Lord knows where,** for I lost sight of her arm. Let the ladies divine, and when their female friends have hysterics, let them profit by the hint; for the remedy operated like a charm, and the young lady's fits ended as fits of young ladies frequently do: she sighed, cried, and grew calm.

From the frequent praises Mrs. Donewell bestowed on her niece, and some hints she gave me, I fancied that she wished me to make honourable addresses to Miss Dinah, whom I judged from her appearance to be a pattern of virtue and modesty, and I began to have myself serious intentions of that kind. One luckless day I walked into the fields with my young landlady, and as the weather was extremely warm, we sat down to rest ourselves in a little wood. My Dinah looked that day more mod-

---

*Vulva. This phrase was a favorite mock-euphemism in the eighteenth century. In 'Hans Carvel,' Prior has a wife furiously telling her husband, 'You've thrust your finger God knows where!'

est, more lovely, and more tempting than ever; insomuch, that wishing to anticipate the smaller chaste pleasures of Hymen, I snatched a kiss or two. Dinah at first called out get *aloong,* let me *alo-one;* but soon after she sunk down softly on the grass. If she was in a fit, it was of a much gentler kind than her hysterics, and though I began as before by giving her room to breathe, my remedies consequently were of a milder nature. With her eyes half closed, she seemed neither asleep nor awake, but in a state between both. I spoke to her, and she did not answer me. I kissed her, and it seemed only to increase her languor. I pushed my attentions further with as little effect, and, as I am naturally an absent man, I forgot it was the chaste Dinah; I forgot it was my future spouse, and treated her as if she had already a right to that title. In the midst of my caresses, she shewed some symptoms of biting, and I feared her hysterics were returning; but on the contrary, in a few moments after she fell into the same sleepy languor as before. Conscious of my fault, I judged that this calm would be succeeded by a storm, the whole weight of which would fall upon my guilty head.

However, as she began to recover her spirits, she pressed my hand with considerable fervency, and at last lifting up her head and giving me a kiss, she exclaimed, *'Behold thou art fair, my beloved, yea thou art pleasant; also our bed is green.'* I found this ejaculation so happily applied, that I could not help lamenting that we had only seven or eight songs remaining of the thousand and five written by King Solomon.

Surprised as I was at her good humour on the occasion, my surprise was still greater three or four days after, when I made the painful discovery of symptoms of a certain disorder, which were by no means equivocal. I flew in a rage to old Mrs. Donewell to acquaint her with her niece's infamy and my misfortune, and supposed that her anger on the occasion would equal mine. She heard me out with the greatest coolness, and answered that, in spite of all I could say, she believed her niece was as modest a girl as any in New-York.

'Besides,' said she, 'if it is true that Dinah has the complaint you mention, it is not her fault, poor thing, somebody has given it to her, and I have no doubt but it is one of those British officers who, according to the words of Ezekiel, are *captains and rulers, clothed most gorgeously, horsemen riding upon horses, and all of them desirable young men —whose flesh is as the flesh of asses, and their issue as the issue of horses.'*

Chapter 6

*Jonathan has the good fortune to
escape with life from a most desperate
action, and the hands of two surgeons.*

As Mrs. Donewell and Ezekiel together
were an over-match for poor Jonathan Corncob, I replied by going to a surgeon: his name was
Bullock, he superintended the naval hospital at
Brooklyn, and was rather a more absent man than
myself. Upon his first coming into the room, he
always addressed me with 'How ar'e?'

After I had detailed all my symptoms, during
which time he generally talked of the wind, and
our military operations, he repeated 'How ar'e?' I
began a second time the sad enumeration, and he a
list of his patients, and an account of the multi-
plicity of his business, which he concluded with
'How ar'e?' At length, after assuring me for a long
half hour that he was in the greatest hurry possible,
he recollected himself, took leave by saying 'How
ar'e?' and disappeared.

The consequence was, that he treated me the

first month as if my disorder had been a putrid fever, and the second as if it had been a bloody flux, giving me cordials instead of refrigerants, and astringents when purgatives were necessary; so that in a short time I had almost all the symptoms of the present Columbus made to Europe: such as gonorrhoea, phymosis, paraphymosis, bubo, sistula in ano, carnositates in uretere, nodi, tophi, gummata, corona veneris, caries ossium, &c. I thought it high time to change my surgeon, and had the good fortune to recover tolerable health, after a long course of frictions, injections, fumigations, scarifications, purgations, salivations, and the like. However, when the cure was completed, I found that I might, in a synagogue or mosque, pass for a Jew or a Turk, but for some cross scores, left by the incision knife, which testified that I was a Christian.

While we were under cure, for Dinah, as well as myself, was in the surgeon's hands, the good old Mrs. Donewell did every thing in her power to pass away the long evenings: sometimes we played at a kind of religious conundrums; as for instance, my old landlady asked, 'What is a deep ditch, and what is a narrow pit?'

Dinah answered instantly, 'A whore is a deep ditch, and a strange woman is a narrow pit.' Mrs. Donewell then asked me 'what was the candle of the Lord, searching the inward parts of the belly?' I blushed at the question, and though I thought it not difficult to divine, was silent. Nobody could answer, till it came to the turn of my dear Dinah, who said 'it was the spirit of a man.' Upon turning to the 20th and 23rd chapters of the Proverbs we found that she had adhered closely to the text.

But as these amusements sometimes grew tiresome, I passed some of the evenings, during my convalescence, at Hull's Tavern. I found there, one day a personage who, though within the British lines, was strongly suspected of favouring the insurgents. He had assumed the post of orator of the coffee-room, and was speaking with great volubility of the King's speech, which had just arrived.

'I remember,' said he, 'when a boy, being at a puppet-show, where Punch was as usual very angry with his wife Joan. He abused her, doubled his fist, and frequently lifting up his leg, menaced her with sounds that resembled the deep notes of a wind instrument. However, Punch's trumpeting did not so exactly imitate nature, but that the difference was perceptible, till in one of his exertions, the sound we heard was so much more mellow, deep-toned, and energetic, that the evidence of our noses corresponding with the information of our ears, a sailor who was present, called out, b——st me, but that's too deep for Punch. So, gentlemen, you may, if you please, call it the King's speech, but I say it is too deep for Punch.'

I was in one of my absent moments, and instead of drinking the rum and water that was before me, I threw pint tumbler and all full in his face. He, with great presence of mind, seized a bottle, and threw it at my head, but, as I had been in a sea action, I bobbed, and the shot passed over me. I ran to the fire and snatching a red-hot poker, made a furious lunge at him in *carte*. He parried it with his arm, by the counter of *tierce,* though not well enough to prevent my running him through the wig, which remained suspended and blazing upon my fiery weapon. He ran in his turn to the fire, and armed himself with a boiler full of scalding water, but as I did not give him time to take off the lid, he was obliged to jerk the water at me through the spout. However he squirted it in my face and breeches with considerable success. Luckily I was next the door, and had the advantage of engaging to windward, so that the smoke of the burning hair and steam of the hot water flew point-blank in his face. I used my poker as a cut and thrust, and singed and carbonadoed him with a vengeance, till the fire having reached the tail of his peruke, I looked like a god armed with a comet, and the enemy could stand it no longer. He ran off, leaving me master of the field of battle, and my scalded legs rendered me incapable of pursuit. So ended an action in which I revenged my insulted sovereign, and which I may without vanity call the *hottest* of the whole war, except perhaps the affair of the floating batteries at Gibraltar. Yet, unpensioned and starved to a skeleton in French Flanders, I may exclaim with Scipio Africanus, '*Ingrata patria ne* OSSA *quidem habebis.*'*

I had, however, the satisfaction of being congratulated on my victory by every body in the coffee-room, and all the persons present pressing me to share their bowls, seemed to wish to stick a sprig of Bacchus's ivy among the laurels of the conqueror. As I have a great share of complaisance,

* 'Ungrateful country, you will get nothing but my bones.'

The hottest action of the war...
M.Livingston del.

they soon succeeded, my head became as infirm as my legs, and in my way home I did not find the *Broad-way* wide enough. I staggered along, still full of indignation against my antagonist, and muttering, at every step, 'The rebel, the sad rebel!' I had not gone far when I stumbled over something, and fell into the kennel.*

Unfortunately the obstacle I met with in my road was nothing less than a sleeping sentinel, who finding himself waked in so rude a manner, thought it was high time to call out, '*Who goes there?*'

In the meantime, I was again on my legs, still repeating as I went along, 'The rebel, the sad rebel!'

The sentinel, provoked at receiving no answer but rebel, and not knowing whether I was one myself, or whether I meant to call him so, supposed in either case that he was justifiable in shooting me, cocked his piece, and fired it without farther ceremony. The whizzing of ball brought me to my recollection; in stooping to avoid it, I fell a second time, with my legs doubled under me, and as I perceived that the sentinel was walking up to me, I thought it prudent to lie still. The sentinel, who, as well as myself, had taken a cup too much, came groping along to discover what had been the effect of this firing, and put his hand on my posteriors, which were wet in consequence of my previous fall in the kennel.

'Dead,' said he, 'dead as the devil—his body is bleeding still. 'Tis comical, d——n'd cau-omical to be sure; I have been in four battles, and at three

*Channel.

sieges, and never saw a man's head shot off by a musket-ball before.' He then retired to sleep on his arms like a good soldier, and as soon as I thought it prudent, I scrambled up, and reached Mrs. Donewell's without any loss, but that of my wig, which in all probability I had left in the kennel.

Chapter 7

A military execution; with the character
of Captain Furnace of the navy.

I REGRETTED this loss exceedingly. I considered the hair that composed it as a relick,
it having belonged to a soldier of a Highland regiment, who was hung at New-York, for stealing, on
a march, two cabbages and three beet-roots, marauding being a capital crime in the military code.

I had been present at the execution of this poor
fellow, and while waiting under the gallows, I remarked to a gentleman standing by me, that I supposed the other delinquents would soon be hanged.
'I did not know,' answered he, 'that there were any
other criminals under sentence.'

'Nor I either,' said I, 'but I heard an officer de-
clare, in a coffee-house last evening, that two army
commissioners, and a navy agent-victualler, had
each robbed government of 100,000£.'

'Oh!' said the gentleman, 'that was the officer's
way of expressing himself, for these supposed rob-

beries consist only in what was formerly called peculation and malversation; but is now expressed by the term perquisite, or as the French call it, *tour de baton.* In the employment of commissary, a man's emoluments are in proportion to his address and good intelligence with the commanding officers. If the public enemy, or a private friend of the commissary, burns a magazine, he makes out an account of double the quantity of stores destroyed, and the commander in chief, who sometimes shares his profits, readily signs his vouchers. An agent-victualler condemns 100,000 sound staves, and 20,000 good iron hoops, as unserviceable, puts them up at auction in the presence of himself, auctioneer, and clerk, and bids 50£ for the lot. The auctioneer knocks them down to the best bidder, who works them up into 1000 ton of cask, and furnishes them to government at 5£ per ton. You see that this is so far from being a robbery *vi et armis,** as in the case of the cabbages and beetroots, that every thing is carried on in the most regular manner possible; and if you think that this way of disposing of the public money is extraordinary, please to recollect that it is precisely for this reason, that the sums voted to answer these demands are called army-extraordinaries, and navy-extraordinaries.'

While my communicative friend was speaking, the culprit made his appearance, attended by the facetious Hibernian who generally presided on these occasions. Nothing could be more entertaining than his manner of acquitting himself of his

*With force and arms.

office. There was none of that gloom, solemnity, and preaching, that is seen at civil executions. This jocular gentleman did every thing in his power to keep the sufferer in good humour. Observing the Highlander look serious while he was arranging the knot, 'Fie, fie! my jewel,' said he, 'you a soldier, used to a leathern stock, and make faces at the touch of a hempen collar! To be sure now, my dear, you are going to be hanged a little, and it will tickle you at first; but in a quarter of an hour you'll not mind it at all at all.' In the midst of his jokes, he took poor Sawney by surprise, pushing him, without the least notice, off the ladder, which he descended himself laughing, and highly pleased at having, as he termed it, taken in the Scotchman.

During the war in America, I was present at the execution of several soldiers, and observed that it seldom happened that a Hessian was punished for marauding. Whenever the troops of that nation saw anything in an American house which suited them, they begged it in a civil way; though at the same time using an argument that was unanswerable—'If you vas one frynd to the Koning,' said Lieut. *Hastendudendrol* of the *Trumbrick* regiment, 'you vas gif me your vatch; if you vas one repell, by Got I take it.'

As soon as my scalded legs were cured, I was ordered to go to Rhode Island, to attend the sale of some plunder landed there, and as His Majesty's ship the *Oddfish* was on the point of sailing, I procured a passage in it to that place. Our voyage was so short, that I had but small opportunities of observing whether the captain was as smart an officer as he who commanded the ship that brought me to New-York. However, an obliging young officer, who seemed to have some penetration, made up the deficiency in my observations. Though what he said was in a kind of confidence, I flatter myself he will pardon my publishing his remarks.

'Nobody,' said he, 'can assert that Captain Furnace is not a seaman, for he d——ns his eyes, chews tobacco, and is an excellent hand at making a sea-pye. He is also allowed to be a good officer, for when it blows hard, he makes more noise than the boatswain and gun-tackles together. When he drinks a great deal of strong grog, which is generally every night, you would suppose the liquor he swallows to be the spirit of contradiction. On the passage to America, whenever he had taken his dose, and we were in the neighbourhood of a rock or shoal, he was sure, spite of all remonstrance, to steer directly for it; and I cannot conceive how we escaped shipwreck, unless, as they say, it is true, that Providence takes care of drunken people. Piquing himself on his resolution and public spirit, he swore that all the gales of wind in the world, all the angels in heaven, and devils in hell, should not drive him off the coast of America, and that rather than bear away for the West Indies, he would *club his ship on the coast,* as he termed it, with *seven cables an end,* though we had only six on board.

'During the last peace, Captain Furnace, who was then a lieutenant on half-pay, resided three years in France, and as he was on an economical plan, boarded in a trademan's family. In consequence of this, he talks much of his French education, fancies

BOTTLED FURY

M. Livingston Del.

himself a nonpareil of politeness, and introduces in his conversation a great number of French words, and French words anglicised. As he has made a particular study of the naval acts of parliament, in which, by way of providing for all possible cases, two or three terms are generally tied together, such as *port or place, ship or vessel,* Captain Furnace generally uses two synonymous words in every phrase, and will tell you that 'last evening or night, when he was going to sleep or repose, he put on his *bonnet de nuit,* or night-cap.'

'Captain Furnace is as brave as any bull-dog; he says so himself, and there is not one of us who has not heard him repeat ten times, and often ten times in the same evening, the account of an action which was so warm, that happening, three hours after it was over, to seat himself astride on a six-pounder, he was scorched to such a degree, that his backside was as raw and as smooth as a singed capon's. Unfortunately he is as quarrelsome as brave. One evening, Mr. Squeeze, our purser, who had staid on shore beyond his leave, coming into his cabin to make an excuse, Captain Furnace stopped him short in his apology. 'What, you are come at last,' said he, 'Mr. Purser, Mr. Judas Iscariot. It seems or appears that you do not *gene* or confine yourself to your duty. G–d strike me d––d, but you have overset or turned the milky bowels of humanity, and blown a degree of rancour into my brain; so get about your business, you son of a b––––'; and without farther ceremony shoved Judas Iscariot out of the cabin. The purser complained to the admiral; the admiral sent for Captain Furnace, who, in his presence, challenged the purser, and threatened to stick his sword in his a——. However, as the admiral talked of a court-martial, unless he begged the purser's pardon in the presence of the officers before whom he had insulted him, Furnace took Mr. Squeeze on board, and having assembled the witnesses, 'Mr. Squeeze,' said he, 'I am ordered or commanded by the admiral, to ask your pardon for having called you a son of a b————. If I must do it, why I beg your pardon; but you are a Judas, and a d——d son of a b————, you know you are.'

'Having heard that one of the midshipmen sometimes intoxicated himself, he sent for him at a time when he had made frequent libations to Bacchus himself, and wishing to make the most awful appearance possible, he had spread on the table in his cabin, a large quantity of acts of parliament. 'Mr. Saunders,' said he, with a hiccough, 'I am told that you sometimes get *tipsy* or *groggy*, which (hiccup!) is very shocking, Mr. Saunders. Drunkenness is a fau-ault I ne-ever will forgive, if I do (hiccup! hiccup!) I hope J–s–s Ch——st never will forgi-ive me.'

'More he would have said, but the weight of the liquor was too much for his legs, and he came down *all four together*, drawing the table upon him, and burying himself in acts of parliament. The quartermaster of the watch and sentinel were obliged to assist in bearing this unwieldy mass to his cot, and Furnace the next day boasted much of his lenity, because he did not punish the midshipman for his want of sobriety.'

After this outline of the character of his commander, the young officer gave me a copy of a conversation he had taken down verbatim, between Captain Furnace; Captain O'Sneak, a half-pay captain of the army, passenger on board the *Oddfish;* and the lieutenant of the ship. I think it hardly necessary to make an apology for inserting it here, as I know my friend the officer has shewn it to several besides myself.

Chapter 8

THE CONVERSATION

The Lieutenant

The loss of Burgoyne's army is really a most unfortunate event.

Captain Furnace

I very naturally prove of the same opinion; but I think General Burgoyne ought to have *ecarted* or withdrawn before he had got so far into the enemy's country: indeed as a military being he ought not to have advanced or proceeded so far without sustenance or provisions for the nourishment of his army; and after all, his own *ospions* or spies ought to have informed or acquainted him of the rebels' approach.

Captain O'Sneak, bowing

Very true, my dear Captain Furnace; if there were always such clear good officers as you, these mistakes would not happen.

Captain Furnace

I am afraid this news will set the people at home

[47]

neck and heels together by the ears very naturally, and that they will prove repugnant to the sending out of any more troops.

The Lieutenant

General Howe's taking Philadelphia is some advantage, however.

Captain O'Sneak

He had no business to take it.

The Lieutenant

I think, Captain O'Sneak, it is rather severe to condemn so hastily, before you know the general's reasons, intentions, or indeed any one circumstance of the campaign.

Captain Furnace

Captain O'Sneak, Captain O'Sneak, I never will allow any degree of censure, while I have the honour very naturally to sit at the head of, or preside at, this table.

Captain O'Sneak

Sir, I most humbly ask your pardon. I never will take that liberty again.

Captain Furnace

Never will, Sir, you never shall. G–d strike me dead, if I allow it, by G–d.

Captain O'Sneak

Sir, I am very sorry—

Captain Furnace

By G–d, Sir, if ever you *ape* or presume to talk in that way again, I'll turn you neck and heels out of my cabin; and if you do not go quietly, I shall order the sentry to stick his bayonet in your a——; if he refuses, I shall very naturally stick my sword in his.

Captain O'Sneak

I hope, Sir, you will never have occasion to do that.

Captain Furnace

G–d strike me d––d, if I suffer any man's character to be injured. The man who takes from me my good name, as Shakespeare says—Sir, I am a justice of peace aboard ship, and can, according to the *lineal* line of service, tie you up and flog you, if you misbehave. My instructions say so, Sir: 'Any person in or belonging to the fleet.' They prove my creed and line of guidance very naturally.

Captain O'Sneak

I never should have ventured the observation, Sir, if I had thought it would have produced any words.

Captain Furnace

By G–d, Sir, you not only insulted me, but yourself, by that observation, and I took notice of it, not that I ape a degree of authority, but because I am, as captain or commander of this ship called *Oddfish,* answerable for the behaviour of everybody in her. I can give you acts of parliament for it, by G––.

Captain O'Sneak

Your authority is certainly very great, Sir.

Captain Furnace

G–– d––– my bl––d, Sir, did you ever know me place or lay a stress or strain upon my authority? No, by G––, if I chose very naturally to expand or extend my authority, you don't know how great it is. Sir, I could flog that officer *(pointing to the lieutenant)* if he disobeyed my orders. No, G––

d——— my bl——d, I could not flog him, but I could
confine him very naturally to his cabin, by G——.
Why, Captain O'Sneak, suppose in case of action,
that I was to order you and the other passengers to
go upon the poop with small arms, and you were
to prove repugnant, you think perhaps, because
you are passengers, that I could not force you; why
G—— strike me dead if I would not very naturally
bayonet every ——— of you.

Chapter 9

*Jonathan meets with a disappointment
in love at Rhode Island; returns to
New-York; meets unexpectedly with
an old acquaintance.*

I LANDED from the *Oddfish* the day after our
arrival, and having a letter from a Loyalist
to his mother, who resided at Rhode Island, I pre-
sented it to the old lady. She insisted upon my
remaining at her house, where I found myself very
agreeably situated. Every evening we played at
Pope Joan,* and at this game I was always in part-
nership with her eldest daughter, a girl of about
seventeen years old. Any other author, who, like
me, had been in love with the lady, would tell you
that the lily disputed with the rose the empire of
her face; that her lips were coral, and her teeth two
rows of oriental pearl; that her nose was well
formed and inclined to the aquiline; that her
large blue eyes were of the sleepy kind, 'that spoke

*A card game with just the right innuendoes. In Pope Joan,
a king and a queen in the same hand are called Matrimony;
a queen and a jack produce Intrigue.

[51]

the melting soul'; that her hair was auburn, and
that she was above the middle size; but I who,
unlike most historians, paint from nature, will
candidly confess that she was a smart little brunette, with sparkling black eyes, and that if she
was not pretty, she was very much to my taste. In
our little commerce at cards, she put our stock of
counters in her lap. Though I am by no means a
miser, I was for ever numbering our riches; and
though I am not naturally a coward, my hand
trembled when it met hers. In a short time the
silent intercourse of eyes and little expressive
larcenies of love, led my passion such a length,
that I almost resolved to lay my share of plunder
at her feet; but when I recollected that the lady's
fortune consisted of twelve silver spoons, tied down
in such a manner, that they could not be taken off
the Island, prudence took the ascendant.

One morning, when I met my Dolly alone, I, like
a true lover, asked her foolishly if she was not cold;
she said no, and to convince me that she was not,
held out her hand; I pressed it in mine, and was
pleased to find the pressure returned. Judging this
a favourable moment, I determined to make a
declaration of love in form—but not in the usual
hackneyed shape of a studied speech—no—any
share that my tongue had in the business did not
consist of words; I pressed my lips to hers, and
under the cover of my kisses made terrible havock
among the out-works of two hemispheres, which,
as my Dolly was a brunette, were not of snow, and
had on me the effect of fire. My fair one made
scarcely any defence, her heart beat upon her lips,

and her passions were in union with mine, when alas! forgive me, reader, if I lay down my pen. Never is the bitter recollection of my disappointment renewed, but I drop a tear; shall sordid souls lament the loss of their useless riches, and the failure of their ill-founded schemes of ambition, and shall not I regret the loss of pleasure, the only good for which we live?—A pleasure too, whose bare recollection would in the chilly season of old age whip on the languid fluids, and light up for a moment the extinguished torch of youth. But let me hurry through the rest;—just as the moment when *big with expectation* I was on the brink of bliss, in came my Dolly's younger sister, to tell her she was wanted in her mother's chamber. She desired me to wait, and returned in a few minutes, but cold as ice; the fever of love had by some means been precipitated to its crisis, and I returned to New-York much afflicted at this disappointment, and little expecting the consolation that awaited me there.

Mrs. Donewell, on my return, grinned very graciously, and Dinah gave me a very tender smile; the former informed me that a whole family of refugees was come to lodge at her house, as well as a captain in a provincial *corps* and his lady. Having many people to see, I left them immediately, and made a variety of visits during the day. In the evening I supped with a Loyalist, who had made a considerable capture of Holland's Geneva. We were only four in number, and after supper he placed two bottles on the table, telling us that he would not give us leave to go till they were finished. As Dinah had told me that she had something to say to me before I went to bed, and as I wished to know what it was, I hasted to dispatch the two bottles; but when they were drunk, two more were produced, attended by the same conditions. In a hurry to be gone I drank the Geneva pure, which disturbed the association of my ideas full as much as the libations I had made on my victory at the coffee-room at Hull's tavern. The night was dark; I went home a very *sober* pace, for fear of accidents; and to be sure of my road, I felt with my hands and head half the door-porches and posts in my way. I let myself in at Mrs. Donewell's, and went as I supposed into Dinah's room. As soon as I was there I was taken with one of my absent fits, and began to undress as if in my own. The getting rid of my clothes was that evening a very tedious operation; I was tugging a quarter of an hour at my breeches, and cursing the tailor for making them so small at the knees, when I discovered that they were still buckled. I could not conceive what prevented my pulling my stockings off, when I found at last that I had forgot the little ceremony of taking off my shoes. I made two or three other blunders, such as the mistaking a flat candlestick for a chamber-pot, and the chamber-pot for a night-cap, and at last rolled into bed. Probably I slept very soundly during the night, but towards the morning I began to dream. Nothing is more true than that a first love is rarely forgotten. I fancied my dear Desire Slawbunk was in my arms, and thought I was caressing her as she merited, when lo! I awoke. I rubbed my eyes, and

"DESIRE!"

M. Livingston Del.

was astonished to find myself with my head at the foot of the bed, and hugging a pair of as pretty feet as a man would desire to kiss. My wonder increased, when I discovered a chamber-pot tied on my head with a worsted garter; but I want a word to express my amazement, when I found my dream realized, and that the feet I had been making love to were those of Miss Slawbunk herself. Yes, a faint light that made its way through the window-curtains, the *softest* of all mouths, and the most languishing of all smiles, convinced me that it was Desire.

'Desire!' said I.

'Jonathan!' said she.

'Good G——!' said I, 'what is all this? the day before yesterday I was in the state of Rhode Island; yesterday in the province of New-York; am I today in Massachusetts-Bay? tell me, for heaven's sake, where I am, my dear Desire.'—And at the same moment I reversed my position, and laid head and chamber-pot upon the pillow of the fair.

Chapter 10

Desire Slawbunk's narrative,
and subsequent conversation.

WHY, I SWEAR NOW, my old acquaintance
Jonathan,' said the lady, 'you are at Mrs.
Donewell's, up two pair of stairs.'

'Heavens!' cried I, 'and how came you here?'

'I will tell you,' said she. 'You know the situation
you left me in—but I will not reproach you. When
I was six months gone with child, a cow I was milk-
ing kicked me down, as well as the pail, and I mis-
carried of a prodigious fine boy, and as like you as
it could stare. Soon after, my father Benaniah Slawbunk set up a tavern, and the British officers, who
were prisoners, dined at our house. Among them
was a Scotch gentleman, captain in a provincial
corps, of the name of Scclear; a tall young man,
though it is true that his height is principally
owing to half an ell of neck; his beard is red, and
his hair black; he is wall-eyed, and his nose has
been rather ill-treated by the small-pox; upon the

whole, as you will suppose, he is not very amiable; notwithstanding he fancied himself pretty, and no lady ever bit her lips or smiled with a greater air of self-complacency. He boasted of himself in every respect, but particularly as to his good fortune with the ladies; however, he was candid enough to confess that his happiness had seldom or never been complete—in numberless instances he had been on the point of succeeding, but had always been prevented by some curst circumstance he had not foreseen; for instance, a want of good-will in the lady, or his unfortunately deferring the attack till the day after he left the place.—He had determined that I should pay for all his disappointments, and made a violent attack on my virtue; taught by experience, I made a good defence, but at last agreed to give him a meeting, of which I meant to inform my father. He, however, had spared me the trouble; he had written a letter to a young man of his acquaintance, desiring him to engage my father in a party at cards while his assignation with me took place. His letter, as I remember, ended in this way:—*Gin you wull obledge me, I wull dow the sam for you:* Seeclear Sedley. It was in consequence of his reputation for gallantry, that he added Sedley to his name. His friend betrayed him, and my father burst into the room when we had been there about a quarter of an hour, and when appearances were much against Seeclear Sedley. The Committee of Safety was consequently assembled, and it was determined, that for the security of the township, the captain should be put in gaol, and forfeit all right to his exchange, unless he married

me. In this dilemma, Seeclear Sedley chose rather
to become a sober husband, and I am now the
captain's lady at your service.

'Last night I saw you come into the room, and
recollected you immediately, but did not choose to
say anything, lest, elevated as you were, your surprise should have occasioned exclamations fatal to
my reputation. I was likewise witness to your
preparations for bed, till a small mistake you made
extinguished the candle; and I tried several times
this morning to wake you, but my efforts were
vain; your sleep was of too sound a kind.'

When Mrs. Seeclear had finished her recital, I
found time to disengage my head from my weighty
night-cap, and to give a few tears to the memory of
my hopeful progeny, cut off by so *untimely* a death.

I then begged Desire to tell me where the captain
was. 'He marched with the detachment that left
New-York yesterday,' said she, 'and commands one
of the flanking parties.'

'A flanking party must be very amusing,' said I;
and the conversation immediately became more
animated.

When our curiosity in respect to each other was
satisfied, I inquired who were the refugees that
lodged in the house. 'What!' said she, 'don't you
know—why I guess it is your own family.'

'Good G——!' said I, 'what, my honoured father
Mr. Habakkuk Corncob?'

'Yes,' said she.

'And my honoured mother Mrs. Charity Corncob?'

'She is here too.'

'And my brother Zedekias, and my brother Hannaniah, and my brother Melchisedeck, and little Jeptha, and my sister Supply, and my sister Increase?—Heaven be praised,' said I, 'here is the whole family of the Corncobs at New-York.'

'My dear Desire,' continued I, 'how they will all be surprised!'

'Not at all,' answered she. 'Mrs. Donewell, after you went out yesterday, told your father that an old lodger of hers and a namesake of his was just come from Rhode Island. He asked a number of questions respecting you, and it was agreed on at last, that you could be no other than his runaway son.'

I went upstairs to my father's apartment, and found the whole family at breakfast. They all started up, and in a moment I was questioned and turned round by every individual: Mr. Habakkuk, Mrs. Charity, my brothers, my sisters, Supply and Increase, every one was eager to hear my adventures, and to see how I looked. All found me improved, and my sister said I was grown handsome. 'Handsome is that handsome does,' said my good old mother Mrs. Charity. This I suppose was meant as a little hint of my depredations in the *store*.

Chapter 11

The misfortunes of Mr. Habakkuk
Corncob.—An American Hunt.—
Jonathan quarrels with
Captain Seeclear.

A s s o o n as I could obtain a moment's silence, I asked my father what events had brought him to New-York.

'I snore now, Jonathan,' said he, 'it was no good luck brought me here. About nine months ago I bought a couple of *creatures* of Colonel Howe, who keeps a tavern at Salisbury. Among the money I gave him for them was a forged fifty dollar bill; it was detected, and information was given to the Committee, which was of opinion, that as I had passed it, I must consequently have forged it, though, as you know, I never could write in my life. The Committee knew it too, but the president had long had an inclination to become possessor of Squatcock farm: I was therefore declared an enemy of the state, all my effects were ordered to be confiscated, and I was sentenced to be set astride on the gallows three different market days. All this was executed, and your poor innocent father was obliged to ride the gallows.'

'I see,' said I, 'that it is the fate of the Corncobs to be oddly mounted; I myself rode sixty miles on a moose deer.'

'However,' continued my father, 'they thought proper to give your mother my hundred acres of land in the neighbourhood of Vermont, for her support and that of the family, while I was lodged in prison. After I had been there three months, I obtained permission to go and tarry three days with my spouse Charity; but as soon as it was known that Corncob the tory was arrived, the whole neighbourhood assembled, and declared, that there was more pleasure in hunting a tory than in hunting a *skunk.** They dragged me directly from the arms of your mother, to whom I had scarcely spoken, and forming a lane according to the laudable custom of the Indians, they made me run the gantlet. When I had got to the end, Lieutenant-General Hand came up, and asked what was the matter. '—We are only giving *considerable of a basting* to this old tory.' 'I swear now,' said he, 'that's *grand*—let him go it again.' I was obliged to run through them a second time, and got off better than could be expected, for I had only my left arm and both collar-bones broke, and my skull fractured. I was more than four months under cure, and as I heard I was threatened with another sample, I contrived to get away, with the

*An American animal, that smells somewhat stronger than a pole-cat.

whole family, and by travelling in the night, by the assistance of our brother tories and God's Providence, we all came safe to New-York.'

When my father had done speaking, I was obliged to give an account of all my adventures; how I lost myself in the wood; how the blue-tailed jays made game of me; how I rode the runaway moose deer; how I was imprisoned at Boston; how I was shoved by the captain of the king's ship, kicked by the lieutenant, and damned by the master; how I was flogged with a cat of nine-tails; how I caught a complaint at New-York; how I was fumigated, salivated, scored and scarified by the doctor; and how I fought a battle at Hull's tavern. My whole relation was heard with the greatest attention, and my gallant behaviour in the battle of the boiler received the warmest applause. My good mother said I should be an honour to the family; even little Jeptha was animated by it, and said he was *full of fight,* and longed to be *blazing away* at the rebels. As to my elder brothers, Zedekias and Hannaniah, the whole of my story had so affected them, that they declared themselves for a roving life. 'If that is the case,' said my father Mr. Habakkuk, 'you have nothing to do but to inlist in the Queen's rangers.'

The whole of us at Mrs. Donewell's continued to live in great intimacy and harmony, except Mrs. Seeclear and Dinah, who did not seem to sympathize, and the captain and I. It sometimes happened, when the captain bit his lips, smiled and looked pretty, that I smiled too. The captain, who was always afraid of being laughed at, did not like

1.ᵉ Act Martial

IVSTITIA   IMPERIVM

2.ᵉ Deliberation Timorous

3.ᵉ Reprisall Politick

THE 3 STAGES OF CHAMBER WARFARE.
Faithfully depicted

M. LIVINGSTON Del.ᵗ

to see anybody laugh unless he knew why; and one evening when I laughed out, as he was a strong powerful fellow, a Scotchman, and a little brutal, he knocked me down. This was the most critical situation I ever found myself in in my life. Nobody but little Jeptha was in the room, and if I returned the blow, I was sure of getting soundly pummelled to no purpose—on the other hand, if I did not resent the injury on the spot, I was convinced that my character for courage would be totally lost. In this perplexing business I fortunately found an expedient, which insured my person and reputation. As a man is supposed to be blinded by rage, I pretended to mistake my little brother Jeptha for my antagonist; I fell upon him, knocked him down, and continued threshing him in good earnest, and abusing him for an overgrown Scotch rascal, till his cries brought half the family from the next room. I then discovered my mistake, and as soon as I found myself held by the arms, wanted to attack the captain, crying out at the same time to my brother, 'What, my dear little Jeptha, is it you I mistook for the scoundrel? I hope, my poor dear fellow, I have not hurt you? How unfortunate it is that my blunder and passion should prevent my chastising the villain as he deserves!'

Although I had declined engaging in a combat of fisticuffs on unequal terms, I was not averse to meeting the captain on fair ground, and sent to demand satisfaction. Captain Seeclear turned a little pale on receiving the message, but soon recollecting himself, he bit his lips, smiled, and said, that though perhaps he had knocked me down, it was never his

intention to offend me in his life, and that nothing
was more disagreeable to him than fighting among
friends, especially where we were surrounded by
enemies.

Chapter 12

*Jonathan goes to Barbadoes, and
is highly satisfied with that island.*

As my youngest sister was extremely pretty, I
was soon after this affair appointed acting
purser of a frigate going to Barbadoes. We very
soon sailed, and had a prosperous passage. When
we were in the vicinity of the West-India islands,
we met at different times more than fifty sail of
ships, none of which we approached, our captain,
who looked at them very attentively, assuring us
always that they were ships of the line. It must be
observed, that we were at this time at war with the
French. Our sailors murmured at being disappointed in their hopes of prize-money, and our sea-
officers, who were used to arithmetic in working
their *day's work,* calculated that the French had
only twelve sail of the line in the West-Indies. The
captain, in short, was blamed by everybody but myself. I endeavoured to vindicate him, and proved
to the officers, that even if he mistook, it was nat-

ural enough, as he always looked through one of Dollond's best six-feet glasses, which magnified exceedingly.

As I knew the climate we were approaching was extremely warm, I fancied that I should find a country totally parched up by the heat, and destitute of foliage and verdure; but when we came within a few miles of Barbadoes, and were sailing round Needham's point, I was astonished at the beautiful appearance of the island. The broad-leaved palm-trees, their stems surrounded with weighty cocoa-nuts; the long lawns well covered with grass, and the white airy houses of the planters, formed a view as picturesque as pleasing, while the romantic highlands of Scotland completed the landscape. 'What a pity,' said I, 'that Barbadoes should be subject to hurricanes!'

No sooner had we cast anchor, than a motley assemblage of inhabitants swarmed on board, composed of all the different shades between the sable African and pale Quadroon, carrying the marks of slavery on their backs, and of content on their faces. They were loaded with the most delicious tropical fruits, poultry, vegetables, and all kinds of refreshments. Our apartment was instantly filled with mulatto girls, almost all of them slaves, yet many of them ornamented with gold necklaces, ear-rings, and bracelets to an amount that would have purchased their freedom, could they have prevailed on themselves to part with their finery. These ladies danced, sung, and caressed us, displaying their talents and their charms, by way of disputing with each other the trifling advantage of washing our linen. When I saw with what good humour they received even a refusal, when I heard the sounds of joviality and joy among our sailors and their black mistresses, and when I had a slice of pine-apple in my mouth, I could not help exclaiming again, 'What a pity that Barbadoes should be so subject to hurricanes!'

The following evening I went on shore, and on going into the coffee-house at Bridgetown, I thought myself in the midst of my acquaintances, though I could not recollect a face I saw. Half a dozen persons together, each a bowl of punch in his hand, crowded round me, and insisted on my drinking. As soon as I had an opportunity of observing them a little, I was of opinion that they had certainly drunk enough themselves, and was no longer surprised at their offering their punch to a stranger, or at their pouring it into his shoes. At any rate the lime punch was excellent, and I could not help saying to myself, that it was a pity such a country should be subject to hurricanes.

A few minutes after, a gentleman came up to me, and asked me if my name was not Corncob. I answered in the affirmative, but said I had not the honour of recollecting him.

'I wonder at that,' said he, 'for we were fellow prisoners at Boston, and made our escape together from gaol.' We immediately began to congratulate and compliment each other.

'Do you remember,' said I, 'the fire on board the English ship that took us aboard?'

'Yes,' said he. He then asked if I remembered the gale of wind on our passage to New-York: I answered yes very faintly, and directly shifted the conversation to some other subject, trembling for fear he should mention my having been flogged. On taking leave he invited me to dine with him the following day, at his plantation, when I was regaled in a most luxurious manner. The turtle was superior to any ever served on a lord mayor's table; the oranges and pine-apples were of the highest flavour; Ben Kenton's porter sparkled like champagne, and excellent claret and Madeira crowned the feast. At the end of the dinner I caught myself unbuttoning my waistcoat, and crying out, 'tis d––d hard that there should be hurricanes in this country.

Towards the evening the gentleman asked me if I would look at his hen negroes. I accepted the proposal, and we walked along a rank of about thirty females of that species. He then asked me how I liked them. I said that perhaps it was owing to prejudice that I did not think them very amiable. After supper he conducted me to my apartment, where I was surprised to find a very pretty mulatto girl. My friend told me, that as I did not seem to like any of his hen negroes, he had sent to a planter of his acquaintance to borrow a beauty of a somewhat lighter hue. I thanked him, told him there was no occasion for such an attention, and expressed my sorrow at his incurring such an obligation on my account.

'Oh!', answered he, 'that is nothing; I shall lend him one of my people to work at his sugar-mill tomorrow, which you know is much the same thing.' Though this extraordinary attention of the West-

Indian shocked the morality of my ideas, yet, as I have always made it a rule to conform to the customs of the countries I visit, I invited the young mulatto girl to get into bed.

'Ki, Ki!' cried the tawny beauty, starting back with the greatest marks of astonishment. Upon my renewing my solicitations, she told me that it was a liberty she could never think of taking; that the mat at the bed-side was destined for her bed; and, 'if massa,' said she, 'want ee chambepot, he will put he hand out of bed; if he want me, he will puttee out he foot.'—There was something droll in this arrangement, but however, it was convenient, and I thought it a thousand pities that Providence should visit so hospitable a country with such frequent hurricanes.

Chapter 13

The West-Indian way of white-
washing, or rather the true way of
washing the blackamoor white.
Jonathan begins to lose his good
opinion of Barbadoes.

M Y F R I E N D took me the following morning to
the house of the planter from whom he had
borrowed the mulatto girl. He was not at home,
but we were, nevertheless, ushered into an apartment, at one end of which was sitting an old
negress, smoking her pipe. Near her was an elderly
mulatto woman; at a little distance was a female
still less tawny of complexion, called in the country,
as I believe, a mestee; and at the other end of the
room I observed a yellow quadroon giving suck to
a child, which, though a little sallow, was as white
as children in Europe generally are. I could not
help remarking to the West-Indian this regular
gradation of light and shade.

'This,' said he, 'is the family of my friend, Mr.
Winter; the three younger females and the child
are the progeny of the old negress.'

'And who are the fathers?'

'Mr. Winter himself is the father of them all,'

replied he: 'when he was very young he had the mulatto woman by the negress: when the mulatto was twelve years old, he took her for his mistress, and had by her the mestee. At about the same age his intimacy with the mestee produced the quadroon, who had by him a few months ago the white child you see in her arms. This is what is called in this country washing a man's self white, and Mr. Winter has the credit of having washed himself white at a very early age, being at this time less than sixty years old.'

This complicated incest, and the coolness with which my friend spoke of it, made me begin to think it no wonder that Barbadoes was subject to hurricanes.

I returned to Bridgetown, and as I had several things to purchase for the use of the ship, I was sometimes obliged to sleep at a tavern there. One morning, when I was sleeping very soundly, I was waked by the most terrible cries of distress. I started up in a fright, supposing it could be caused by nothing less than a hurricane, slipped on my breeches, the hind part before, put my right arm into the left sleeve of my coat, and ran downstairs. I found below two ill-looking negroes, who were flogging two young negresses stripped entirely naked, while the tavern-keeper superintended the operation, and proved himself no bad anatomist, by pointing out the most sensible parts. The two poor girls interrupted their cries between each lash to call out to the inn-keeper, 'Oh! Oh! good massa'; and, 'Dammee heart,' to their black executioners.

'What is the matter?' said I, to the master.

'Nothing in particular,' said he. 'It is the last day

Mr. Winter's Family, OR
the West Indian Way of White-Washing.

M. Livingston Delt.

of the month, when I always make it a rule to give a few lashes to my slaves, otherwise, look'e, Sir, they would not be worth a squeezed sugar-cane. However, nobody on the island is more humane than I am; I am not one of those who flog for flogging's sake, and without reason or bounds. I always observe the mosaical law, and give exactly forty stripes save one.'* As these reasons were unanswerable, I returned to my bed, and left him to make up the number, though I could not help muttering, as I went upstairs, that a good hurricane would be no bad thing at Barbadoes.

The same day I met with two officers of my acquaintance, who asked me to go with them to a ball, given by an inhabitant of Bridgetown. I consented readily to be of their party, though I afterwards repented of my complaisance, on observing that they had both taken rather too large a dose of Madeira. We went into the ball room, engaged partners, and all went on very well for about half an hour, when the lady with whom Lieutenant Dasher, one of my friends, was dancing, dropped a garter. The lieutenant, who was a very polite man, picked it up, and offered to put it on. The young lady blushed, and begged to be excused. Her brother, a creole, who was standing by, interposed, and pointed out to the lieutenant the impropriety of his offer. However, my friend insisted, with some reason, that the lady could not dance with her stockings about her heels; that he was her partner, and that as nobody knew better how to

*Thirty-nine lashes, the same number as the Thirty-nine Articles of Religion in the Church of England.

put on a lady's garter, he had an exclusive right. The brother denied it.

'Pshaw,' said Lieutenant Dasher, with a hiccough, 'you're drunk, Sir,' and stooping down, prepared to put an end to the debate.

The brother took him by the arm to prevent him, but my friend catching him by the leg, threw him on his back. In an instant half a dozen creoles ran up to his assistance; the lieutenant drew his sword, at the sight of which two ladies fell into hysterics, three begged permission to faint, and four called for smelling bottles. The number of creoles increased, the lieutenant was disarmed, another officer and myself joined him, and the battle became general; but as they were thirty to three, we attempted to make a handsome retreat and gain the door. We should have succeeded if our ill-fortune had not placed a curst musician in the door-way, who seeing our design, stopped me, who was in the front, by thrusting the reed-end of his clarinet into my mouth. I attempted to draw back my head, but the crowd behind prevented me, and I continued jammed up in this situation for several minutes, with the wind instrument in my mouth; every thump I received from the enemies producing a note high or low, agreeable to the part on which the blow fell, and I played such a piece of involuntary music as I believe was never before heard. At last, however, our efforts got the better of the clarinet player, and we descended the staircase with great precipitation.

As soon as we were at the bottom of it, we desired a parler, and offered to fight any of the combatants,

man to man. The creoles told us, that they were
rather inclined to dance at that moment, but that
they would settle the matter the following morning. The following morning we waited on them
all, and were astonished at their assuring us
severally, that so far from having ill-treated us, they
had interposed in our favour; that they had received blows intended for us, and each of them in
particular declared upon his honour, that but for
his interference we should certainly have been
killed. As we could not insist upon fighting with
people to whom we had such great obligations, we
were obliged to be content with our threshing, and
to leave our revenge to the next hurricane.

This adventure gave myself and fellows in misfortune but little taste for the society of the Bar-
badians, and we rather chose to pass our evenings
in strolling about the vicinity of the town, than at
the balls and concerts of the inhabitants of Bridgetown. In one of our walks our attention was attracted by the appearance of something black under
a hedge, which, on examination, we found to be a
negress. This hapless creature was lying on the bare
ground, in the last agonies of a burning fever. Her
whole body was covered with sores and pustules,
caused by the bites of the flies and musquitos, that,
from the freedom with which they preyed on her
person, seemed to insult her defenceless situation.
The remnant of a blanket about her waist was her
only covering, and a little dirty water in the bottom of a broken pitcher the only nourishment
within her reach. Her eyes, though already covered
with the film of death, seemed to implore our as-

sistance.—We ran to a neighbouring house to learn the reason of her being there, and were told by a woman, that she was the slave of a planter, that her master fearing she might communicate the fever to his other negroes, had brought her to die under the hedge, and that she had already been there three days unnoticed by anybody, and without any sustenance but the water in the pitcher. As she told us, that without a sum of money it was impossible for us to give, nobody would afford her a lodging, we proposed to leave some provisions by her, but the woman assured us that the other negroes would not fail to steal them immediately. We were devising other means to assist the sick slave, when giving a last groan, and expiring, she left us nothing to do but to wish her a better fate in another world. Lieutenant Dasher proposed setting fire to Bridgetown, but I begged him to leave the punishment of this Barbadian cruelty to the next hurricane.

Chapter 14

*A hurricane at Barbadoes, and
an account of the damage caused by it.*

O UR SHIP being ordered to prepare for sea, I
went to say farewell to my friend the planter
who received me with his usual hospitality. After
having been treated during the day in the most
luxurious manner, in the evening I retired to bed;
the little mulatto girl being as usual stretched out
on her mat by the bed-side. Soon after we both fell
so fast asleep, that we could not hear ourselves
snore. I, for my own share, was dreaming of nothing less than a hurricane, when I was waked by the
falling of the Venetian blinds and sashes into the
room. I started up in my bed, and opening my
mouth to call out murder! thieves! the wind rushed
in so furiously, that I could not shut it again. I
then began to suspect what was the matter, and was
not a little alarmed at the rocking of the house. I
was in doubt what step to take, and was much
afraid I should be buried in the ruins of the build-

ing, when the mulatto girl took me by the arm, and
pulled me towards the opposite window. 'One
cursee hurricane to be sure,' said she; ' but good
little *macky** blue-coat, never be afraid.' She then
lowered herself down by her hands, and jumped to
the ground. I followed her example, and jumped
upon her back. The girl immediately recovered her
legs, and, driven on by the wind, ran along at an
amazing rate. As my good fortune had placed me
on her back, I thought proper to keep my hold, for
as she was in the front, it was clear that she would
first encounter any obstacle in the way, and save
my bones at the expence of her own. This reasoning, as she was a slave, was very fair; but the wind
and my weight soon became too much for her; she
fell upon her face, and I was dismounted. I continued to be carried on by the wind with the greatest swiftness, and was much afraid I should be
driven to sea, where in all probability I should have
been lost, when I was suddenly taken off my feet,
and falling from a considerable height, found myself very happily seated in a kind of ravine that was
sheltered on every side. During my journey the
wind had blown my shirt piece-meal off my back,
and when I got into shelter, I perceived that I had
nothing but the collar and wristbands left to cover
my nakedness. There was a very numerous company in this hollow way, which was every moment
increased by stragglers, who came flying in upon
our heads, till at last we were crowded one upon
another, and almost stifled with excessive heat.
Terrible were the complaints on every side of me,

*A mack is a pimp. The term is still current in Black English.

every one enumerating his supposed losses, and lamenting his friends killed, or supposed to be killed. 'My poor wife!' cried one; 'my poor dear boy!' exclaimed another.

As I had heard that the best way of consoling our fellow-creatures, is to divert their attention from their misfortunes, by relating our own, I began to cry out, 'Oh! my poor dear blue coat! my best white dimity waistcoat! my new prince's stuff breeches!' A planter, who was standing near me, and who was probably in a bad humour at being blown out of bed, imagined me to be making game of him; he fell upon a creole lady whom, in the dark, he mistook for me, and pummelled her till her cries, and some discoveries he made in the action, undeceived him. When I perceived what was the matter, I left off my lamentations, and shifted my place to another, where, though I was safer, I was not near so much at my ease. I found myself in the middle of a company that did not seem to be of the most cleanly kind, at least if I could judge from the strong smell of perspiration that almost suffocated me. As soon as the day began to dawn, perceiving that I was in the midst of six overgrown negresses, I begged these black natives of Congo to give me a little room, 'for really,' said I, 'my good women, you smell very strong.'

'Fie, fie, massa,' answered one of them, 'what we smell! ee fair sex smell! 'tis ipposible—no—neber see de day dat ee fair sex smell.' I made my way from among these sable fair ones, and went up to two young ladies of my acquaintance, whom I observed at a little distance, and who were as totally

naked as myself. I made them a very ceremonious
bow, they returned full as formal a courtesy, which,
in the situation they were in, had so comical an
effect, that I could not help laughing. The ladies,
suspecting the cause of my mirth, turned their
backs upon me, an expedient that by no means
lessened my merriment. However, as I observed
that my laughter seemed to displease some of the
people about me, who were almost all naked too, I
changed my tone, and began to comfort those that
appeared to be the most in want of consolation.
There was one planter in the number, whose sorrow was more turbulent than that of his neighbours. He roared, sobbed, cursed the hurricane,
and called himself the most unfortunate of men.

I went up to him. 'Sir,' said I, 'consider we are
all mortal, and if your wife had not met with this
misfortune, she must have died sooner or later.
Your sorrow, my good sir, cannot bring her back.
Besides, she is, no doubt, in heaven; where, according to the best accounts, she must be better off,
than we poor, naked Christians in this nasty ravine.

'What do you mean, Sir?' said he, still sobbing;
'my wife is the lady whom you see just by.'

'I beg your pardon for my blunder,' replied I,
'but if you have lost your children, do not let it
afflict you too much; it is a loss your lady, who is
still young, can easily repair.'

'Children, Sir!' said he, 'I never had any in my
life.'

'Oh!' said I, 'I see what is the matter, your crop
of sugar is destroyed, and your house blown down.'

'Oh! no, no, no,' answered he, 'that house yonder

is mine. Oh, oh, oh! I left it last night, for fear it
should fall; but I see that it is safe, and my crop of
sugar is all housed.'

'For G–d's sake, what is the matter then?'

'Oh, oh, oh!' said he, sobbing still louder, 'Oh,
oh, oh! I have lost twenty negroes, and six of them,
oh oh, oh!'—here his tears interrupted his voice—
'Oh, oh, oh! six of them were she's, oh, oh, oh! and
big with young, oh, oh! I would not have sold them
for fifty *Jos* a-piece.'*

A few hours after day-break, the wind became
moderate, and naked as we were, we determined to
leave the ravine, to inquire after our respective
friends. I directed my steps towards the house of
my acquaintance the planter, which I was overjoyed to find standing. He had left it in the night,
as well as myself, but was just returned, and had
the kindness to supply the loss of my shirt. From
the plantation we went to Bridgetown, which was
no more than a heap of ruins. An infinite number
of its inhabitants were carried off by various accidents, and a few days after, the following list of the
victims of the hurricane appeared at Bridgetown:

Men, women, and children, buried beneath
the ruins of buildings 527
Drowned 134

Total 661

Loss of black cattle.

Oxen lost by different casualties 745
Which, with 4273 head of negroes, ... 4273

Makes the amount 5018

*A jo or joe was a gold coin worth about nine dollars.

Chapter 15

*Jonathan returns to New-York, where
he is appointed purser of an armed
brigantine. Meets at sea with the
Picaroon American privateer. The
captain of Jonathan's brig obliged to
strike, the commander of the
Picaroon being one of the most
obstinate fellows upon record.*

L U C K Y was it for me that I had a friend in the
kind planter who had been formerly my fellow prisoner. My ship was blown to sea, and was
never afterwards heard of. During four months that
I waited in hopes of its return, he insisted on my
staying at his house. At the expiration of that time,
I took a passage in a merchant ship to New-York,
where I was received with open arms by the whole
family of the Corncobs, Mrs. Donewell, and Dinah,
who had all supposed me lost in the hurricane.
Very soon after, I was appointed purser of an
armed brig in the service of government. Our commander was Captain Quid, who was reputed a very
brave officer, and whose conversation soon convinced me that he merited his reputation. Our brig
mounted fourteen guns, and, during the time it

was sitting out, lay along-side a polacre* in government service, that mounted sixteen.

'That's a fine little ship,' said I, one morning, to Captain Quid.

'Pooh!' said Captain Quid, 'I wish I had nothing else to do than to take such a one every day before breakfast.'

A few days after, we sailed on a cruise, and, after having been a week at sea, fell in with a sail, to which we gave chase. Everybody on board was overjoyed.

'Let me see,' said the lieutenant, 'a French West-Indiaman cannot be well worth less than sixteen thousand pounds. The master and I have an eighth between us: that makes my share a neat thousand; a pretty good beginning this, though to be sure it is a pity we commission officers should not have a better share.' As we approached the ship of which we were in chase, and which likewise directed its course for us, I observed our captain walk very hastily up and down the deck, taking a look with his glass at every turn. At last he called the master.

'Master,' said he, 'it is a very large ship that, see what you make of her.'

'O Lord!' said the master, 'what an ugly row of teeth she has!'

'How many guns do you count?' said Captain Quid.

'She carries sixteen, at least, Sir,' answered the master.

'All hands about ship!' cried the captain. Up

*Or polacca. A three-masted, lateen-rigged ship, once widely used in the Mediterranean.

came the lieutenant, the gunner, the boatswain, two boatswain's mates, three quarter-masters, and four midshipmen: all began to give directions.

Since the death of Stentor and Whitfield, never was such bawling heard. I was so stunned by the speaking trumpets that I am a little deaf of the right ear to this day. However, all our exertions were vain; the ship outsailed us, and was soon along-side.

'*What ship's that?*' cried out the captain of the strange sail.

Captain Quid put the speaking trumpet to his mouth, and answered 'Boo-o-o.'

'*What ship's that?*' said he, in his turn.

'Boo-o-o-o,' said the other. This conversation was repeated, by way of question and answer, for a quarter of an hour, when Captain Quid observed that he never had met with so obstinate a fellow; 'but to be sure,' said he, 'as he has sixteen guns, and we only fourteen, I must answer him. *The* Despair *brig*,' said our captain.

'*Hoist out your boat*,' said the other.

Captain Quid put the speaking trumpet again to his mouth, and called out, '*Hoist out your boat.*'

The captain of the other ship repeated the request; Captain Quid did the same, and I thought they would never have been tired of saying the same thing; till at last the other commander called out, 'Hoist out your boat, or d––n you, I'll sink you.'

'I have been at sea forty years, man and boy,' said Captain Quid, 'and never met with so obstinate a fellow; but as he has sixteen guns, and we only fourteen, hoist out the boat.'

The lieutenant went on board the strange ship, the captain of which, as soon as he had the boat's crew in his possession, called out, 'Strike to the Picaroon *American privateer.*'

Our captain asked the officers what was to be done. 'Master,' said he, 'that ship outsails us.'

'Yes, Sir.'

'We cannot get off then,' said Captain Quid. 'Gunner,' continued he, 'there is so much sea, that if you were to fire, you could not hit the enemy.'

'No, Sir,' said the gunner, 'not very well, and I do not believe that he could hit us.'

'It is clear then,' said Captain Quid, 'that as he has sixteen guns, and we only fourteen, we have nothing to do but to strike—hey! don't you think so?'

Before the officers could answer, a voice called out from the other ship, 'Be brisk in hauling down your colours, or I'll send you to d— nat——n.'

'O Lord! what an obstinate fellow!' said our captain. 'Quarter-master, haul down the colours.'

When we came on board the *Picaroon,* we found everybody highly pleased at the complaisance of our captain. I thought myself it was a pity he had not been more obstinate, especially when the pilot of the privateer told me, that they only waited for our firing, to strike, having no intention of fighting a king's ship, which from its superior discipline must have had the best in an engagement. 'That may be true,' said I; 'but unfortunately you had sixteen guns, and we only fourteen, and your captain is a terrible obstinate fellow.'

I was then introduced to the purser of the *Picaroon,* who, as his brother officer, gave me a very civil reception, and begged a sight of the little baggage I had brought on board. 'Your bedding,' said he, ordering a sailor to take it up, 'is considerable nice bedding, and according to the *rudiments* of the navy, I guess it belongs to me. Your clothes and linen are in that trunk, I suppose?'

'Yes,' said I.

'How many shirts are there?'

'Two dozen.'

'I swear now,' said he, 'that's grand,' making a sign to his boy to carry the trunk into his cabin; 'but,' added he, 'if you should tarry ten or twelve days on board, before we get into port, and should want a change of linen, I'll lend you a shirt with all my soul, for I swear now I am always glad when I can assist a brother officer in distress.'

We were all carried into Boston harbour, and put on board the King's Town prison-ship, where I was much afraid of being known; but as I was grown taller, and wore my own hair, nobody I met with, while prisoner, recollected me. The captain, the other officers, and myself were ushered into the great cabin. We found this apartment worthy of its name, being by exact admeasurement 9 feet, 10¾ inches long, and 8½ feet broad. Our number, when added to that of the people already in it, amounted to twenty-two; we were consequently not much at our ease, and when bed-time came, were much embarrassed to find room to dispose of our persons. After a great deal of bustle and dispute, I found a spare plank, on which I stretched myself, and no sooner was my head on the pillow, as the saying is, then I fell fast asleep. I was soon after waked by a dozen voices, that made a most confounded noise in calling out for silence. When silence was obtained, one of them, addressing the captain of a West-Indiaman, desired him to say prayers. 'With all my heart,' said the other, and executed his pious office in these words: 'O L——d our father, which art in heaven, of thy infinite goodness and mercy, look down, and d——n, c——se, bl——t, blow, burn, blind, sink, and utterly destroy the thirteen united states of America.' All the audience said *amen!* with great fervour, and we composed ourselves to rest.

However, spite of our prayers, we did not pass a quiet night. About the middle of it, we were alarmed by a hoarse roaring, interrupted by efforts like those of a man choaking. Over our heads was a guard of sixteen militia-men, who had, either by accident or design, overset a certain utensil, which must have been very capacious, for its contents came pouring through the seams in the deck, in large streams. Captain Quid always slept on his back, and with his mouth open, which at this moment was exactly under one of the largest cracks in the deck, consequently one of the largest currents flowed directly into it, and occasioned the vociferation and sputtering that waked us. The rest of us soon had our shares of this savoury jest, and the indignation became general. 'By the L——d,' said Captain Quid, 'if anybody will join me, we will go up and throw the rascally guard overboard.'

Immediately twelve others and myself jumped up, and armed ourselves with billets of wood, furnished us for the purpose of dressing our victuals.

The other eight were so fast asleep, that all the means we made use of to wake them, were ineffectual; although several of them had spoken just before we proposed throwing the guard overboard. As soon as we were all ready, I begged Captain Quid to put himself at our head; 'But Sir,' said I, 'they are sixteen to fourteen.'

'Very true,' answered he, 'I never thought of that, and I am of opinion, that we had better go to bed again; but, gentlemen, you may take my word for it, that things shall not go on in this manner; I'll take care of that: for as I am a man and an officer, I'll—I'll talk to the guard, and beg them not to overset their chamber-pot again, for I would as soon be p–ssed upon, as be treated in this way.'

Chapter 16

Jonathan's sad reflections in gaol:
meets with an alarm, which
terminates agreeably.

———————

THE FOLLOWING day the deputy of the deputy commissary of prisoners brought on board our provisions, which consisted of a little bad rice, and damaged salt beef, that had been condemned as good for nothing but to be given to prisoners. As it smelt very strong, I could not help turning up my nose. The deputy of the deputy commissary of prisoners thought I turned up my nose at him, and as he was a person of importance, being cobbler by profession, and major in degree, he ordered the guard to carry me to the gaol at Boston. The gaoler gave me a very civil reception, and, with two of his attendants, conducted me to my apartment, where I observed a long iron bar, fastened down to the floor. The gaoler said he was under the necessity of searching me; but begged me to excuse him. He found my purse in my pocket; put it in his own, and assured me that I should want for nothing where I was, the state allowing me a pound of bread per day, and as much water as I chose to drink. 'Your shoe-buckles,' said he, taking them out of my shoes, 'would make your feet uneasy in these rings.' He then locked my feet in two rings, that were rivetted to the bar of iron. 'Your wrists,' added he, 'would be apt to gall if you kept your sleeve-buttons in your shirt.' He therefore took them out, confined my hands in two more rings, that like the former were rivetted to the bar of iron, and took leave, desiring me to amuse myself in any way I thought proper. As my hands and feet were so close together, my nose consequently was not far from my knees, a kind of posture that is not very easy. At the end of eight and forty hours, I was not at all reconciled to my situation. I fell insensibly into a train of dreary ideas, and taking a review of all that had happened to me in two years, I could not help thinking myself the most disastrous wight in existence. Obliged to fly my country for the first little mistake I ever made in bundling; flogged by the first captain of the navy I ever saw; and p–xed by the first woman I ever intended to make my wife: surely, said I, no man was ever so ill-treated by his evil genius as I am. I have since been beat at Barbadoes; almost choking with the reed-end of a clarinet; blown naked out of bed in a hurricane; p–ssed upon by the guard of a prison-ship; and to crown all, here I am with my legs and wings pinned down like a trussed pullet's. However, courage, friend Jonathan! the kind hand of Providence will, no doubt, as usual, take you out of this scrape—to help you into another. In this state of resignation, and with my chin between my knees, I fell asleep. Towards midnight, as near as I can guess, I felt my elbow jogged, and waking suddenly in a fright, cried out as is customary in all such cases, murder! thieves!

'Jonathan!' said a voice that seemed close to my ear.

My fright redoubled; but conceiving it to be a spirit, I exclaimed '*In the name of the Father, Son, and Holy G—st, what art thou?*'

'Make no noise,' said the voice, 'I am in the next room.'

I began to take courage when I heard that, and called out with great firmness: '*In the Devil's name who are you?*'

'Wait a little,' answered the voice, 'and you shall know.' During two or three hours after, I heard a continual scraping and scratching against the side of the wall. At last three or four bricks fell into the room, and I felt a soft, warm feminine face in contact with my own.

'Kiss me, Jonathan,' said the person.

'The order is not disagreeable,' said I; and I directly did as I was desired. A peculiar softness in the mouth, and a peculiar energy in the lady's manner of kissing, brought my own country, I could not tell why, to my remembrance; which, by the same unaccountable concatenation of ideas, called back to my recollection a farm-house, adjacent to my father's. The idea of the farm-house was attended by that of a bed; and that of the bed made me think of my dear Desire Slawbunk.—It was herself, and I leave the reader to judge of our kind congratulations, and sad condolences. When they were over, I asked her by what accident she was my neighbour in the prison. Desire, with great prudence, begged me to suspend my curiosity, and drawing back her head, continued to work at the wall till she had made an opening large enough to admit her body to pass. She then came into my apartment, and as it was already day-break, she hid the bricks and mortar in the chimney, and covered the vacancy they had left with a chair, that it might escape the observation of the gaoler.

Chapter 17

Mrs. Seeclear's narrative.—
Jonathan in a great danger
experiences the efficacy of prayers.

A s s o o n as this was arranged, Desire seated herself by me on the floor, and began thus. 'You
remember that you left me three months ago at
Mrs. Donewell's, at New-York. A few days after,
my poor dear husband, Captain Seeclear, was surprised by the rebels on an out-post.' Here the tears
bedewed Mrs. Seeclear's cheeks. When she had
cried three minutes, the space of time decency di-
rects a widow to weep, on mentioning her husband
in the three first months of her widowhood, she
smiled kindly on me and continued.

'I was unfortunately with him, and we were carried off prisoners together. An Irishman, who had
deserted from Rawdon's legion, was appointed to
guard my husband and myself. My charms, which
from that moment I have detested, made an im-
pression on him, and he insisted on violating my
honour in the presence of my husband. Captain

Seeclear, in his polite manner, which you may remember, smiled, bit his lips, represented in civil
terms to the Irishman the brutality of his intention,
and finished by observing that it was unworthy of
a soldier to injure the wife of an officer who had
seen service, and at whom a bushel of musket-balls
had been fired.

'The Irishman immediately seized his musket:
'By Jasus,' said he, 'perhaps they did not give you
good measure, so there is another to make it up';
and at the same instant shot the poor captain in
the neck. He was immediately taken with a rattling
in his throat, and expired a few moments after,
Desire being the only word he was able to pro-
nounce.'

Here Mrs. Seeclear's tears began to flow again,
but after three minutes she composed her countenance and went on.—'I was so intimidated by
what I saw, that I no longer opposed any resistance
to the intentions of the Irishman, who triumphed
over my virtue. You, my dear Jonathan, may easily
imagine what my feelings must have been on such
an occasion.'

'It is not at all difficult to divine what they were,
madam,' answered I a little angrily; 'but pray go
on.'

'He afterwards proposed to me to live with him;
I did not know how to refuse, besides, the greatest
mischief was already done. A fortnight after, a part
of his regiment was defeated by a few British
troops. My Irishman might, in all probability, have
escaped, if he had not unfortunately been taken
prisoner by a dragoon's horse.'

'How the devil!' said I, interrupting her, 'taken prisoner by a dragoon's horse! You must certainly mean by a dragoon.'

'I know very well what I say, Sir,' answered she; 'he was seized by the shoulder and made prisoner by a dragoon's horse that had lost its rider. I had my information from a person on whose veracity I can depend.'

'Oh!' said I, 'that alters the case; I beg your pardon, my dear Desire; but pray proceed.'

'Where did I leave off?' said she.

'At your friend's being taken prisoner by a dragoon's horse.'

'True,' continued Desire, 'and immediately after he was hung as a deserter. Though he beat me regularly once a day, there was something so affectionate in his manner of making peace at night, that I could not help regretting his loss. I afterwards fell into the hands of a Hessian corporal, who was likewise a deserter. This gentleman put a basket on my back, filled it with potatoes, cabbages, plunder, and a camp kettle, and made me march till I fainted with fatigue, while he walked by my side with all the majesty possible, his pipe in his mouth, and his cane hanging upon one of his coat buttons.

'I was soon tired of being a Hessian's *bât* horse, and made my escape one night when there was an alarm in the camp, and when one half of the army was running away without their breeches, and the other half putting them on. I was scarcely at the distance of four miles from the American army when I met with a party of British sailors, who had

landed with the intention of carrying off a few
sheep and a little hay. They had been unsuccessful
in their schemes of plunder, but the lieutenant,
who commanded them, and who had a wife and
daughter at Saltash, was determined that his expe-
dition should not be fruitless, and plundered me
of my cap and black silk hat and cloak.

'A few days after I reached Boston, where I found
a cousin of my poor dear husband, prisoner in the
apartment I now inhabit. As he made his escape
from gaol a few days after, I was suspected of having facilitated his evasion, and was ordered by the
president of the council, Mr. Powell, to be tarred
and feathered, as an enemy of the state. I was
stripped naked, tarred, rolled in a great quantity
of turkey's feathers, and had made about half the
circuit of Boston, when a butcher's dog mistaking
me for a bear, seized me, and tore away half my
right breast. The butcher, who was a charitable
man, by way of making me amends, took me to his
house, and expended a hundred weight of hog's
lard in freeing me from the tar, which, however, I
did not get rid of without the loss of a great part
of my skin. I was not yet cured of my wound and
excoriations, when the act of retaliation took
place, and I was sentenced, in consequence of it, to
inhabit the apartment from which it was supposed
I had helped to deliver my relation. Before I had
got a new skin on my face the gaoler was very
brutal; but since I have begun to recover my good
looks, his behaviour is totally altered, and he treats
me with great attention and kindness. It was from
him I heard that Mr. Corncob, purser of the

Despair brig, was in prison. As soon as I had this information I employed an old sharp-pointed poker to make a hole in the wall, and it was this poker that jogged your elbow, and caused your alarm on your first waking from your sleep.'

Scarcely had Desire finished her narrative, when we were alarmed by the creaking of bolts and hinges. She instantly darted through the hole in the wall, and drew the chair against it in such a way as to conceal it perfectly. An instant after, my door was opened, and the gaoler and the deputy of the deputy commissary of prisoners made their appearance, attended by a little wounded American officer, hopping on crutches.

'Gentlemen,' said I, 'you'll excuse my rising.'

'Oh! don't mention it,' answered the commissary; 'I am always attentive to the prisoners under my care, and as I do not suppose you are perfectly at your ease, I am come to propose to you to ask my pardon in the presence of this officer; on this condition I will permit you to return to the prison-ship.' I told the deputy of the deputy commissary of prisoners, that, as I was conscious of no fault, I could not possibly think of asking pardon.

'Very well,' said he, 'I *snore*, then, I'll leave you there to rot': and was going away, when the gaoler interposed, and observed, that if my offence was not very great, he thought I had been sufficiently punished.

'A pretty impertinent fellow of a gaoler!' said the wounded officer.

The gaoler answered so insolently to this exclamation, that the wounded officer, seizing his left crutch in his right hand, applied it to the most prominent part of the gaoler's face. The gaoler, finding his nose bleed, hesitated a moment to consider what was to be done, stepped back two paces, and with as much coolness as ever I saw in a man in my life, drew his—handkerchief out of his pocket, and wiped the blood off his face. Then, supposing himself at a pretty safe distance from the crutch, he began to renew his invectives. 'A fine feat you've done,' said he, 'to be sure—you have broke the nose of a father of a family, but, you little puppy, lay down your crutch, and I have a boy of twelve years old, who shall put you on his knee and flog you.'

This sarcasm on his size wound up the passion of the mutilated hero to such a height, that, hopping on one crutch, he pursued my very good friend the gaoler with the other. The gaoler very prudently dodged round me, and avoided the crutch with great dexterity, but alas! I was not so fortunate, all the blows meant for him fell on my head, for pinned down as I was, I could neither escape nor parry them, and I considered my last hour as present. I could not at all digest the idea of being killed by such an old woman's weapon as a crutch, so, as an only resource, I determined to say my prayers, and began with the litany. The little wounded officer, frustrated in his hopes of vengeance, hopped after the gaoler with greater speed than ever; the gaoler skipped round me with proportionable activity; the blows redoubled on my head, and I hurried on through the litany with all possible dispatch.

Jonathan mis-taken

M. Livingston Delt.

I was just come to the part 'from battle, murder, and sudden death, good Lord deliver us,' when my prayers were heard, and I was preserved for fresh misfortunes. Desire having been employed all night in making the hole in the wall, on her retreat to her own room had begun to undress, with the intention of going to bed; but judging from the blows she heard, and from my muttering my prayers, that somebody was murdering me at least, her concern for me was more powerful than her fears or her modesty, and she rushed naked through the opening in the partition, overturning in her way the commissary, who was seated in the chair that masked the wall, and who had, with great tranquility, been a spectator of the affray.

Desire, naked as she was, fell over the commissary, and, by way of breaking her fall, caught the gaoler by the leg, and pulled him down upon her. The little officer, unable to stop himself, fixed his crutch on the backside of his enemy, but having awkwardly applied it to the convexity instead of the concavity, it flipped, he fell upon the gaoler, and when down, like Witherington on his stumps at Chevy Chase,* distributed his blows with great courage and effect. Desire was the first who disengaged herself, and when on her legs, both tails of her shift being torn off, attracted the intention of the combatants, who, lying on their backs, were struck with wonder at this apparition, and sus-

---

*Richard Withrington, a Northumberland squire, is said to have lost both legs at Chevy Chase in 1388, and to have continued fighting against the Scots anyway. He is celebrated in the ballad of *Chevy-chace*.

pended all hostilities. The commissary profited by
the opportunity to make peace between the gaoler
and lame soldier, and as I had suffered consider-
ably in the action, I was included in the amnesty.
The gaoler unlocked my legs and arms, and proposed to give us all a breakfast. While it was pre-
paring, Desire stepped into her own room to dress,
and I related our meeting of the night before.

After breakfast, the commissary ordered the
gaoler to allow me all the indulgence possible, and
said he hoped soon to bring me news of my exchange. He then took leave, and retired with his
friends, leaving me to console myself in the em-
braces of my chaste Desire.

Profiting by the privileges of an old acquaintance, I passed the nights regularly in her room, till
one day she desired me to stay in my own. I asked
her why; she said she had reasons to desire my
absence; and, as I did not wish to scrutinize feminine mysteries, I no longer insisted. In the evening
I heard the gaoler come into the room, at a later
hour than usual, and from the whispers and mur-
muring I overheard, I could not help suspecting an
intelligence between them, which was sufficient to
make a jealous man uneasy.

About an hour after I heard the door of Desire's
room open suddenly, and was not long in doubt as
to the person who made the visit. '*O the nasty
rogue! O the nasty hussey!*' cried out a shrill
female voice. 'I vow I'll tear her eyes out.' The
gaoler's wife, in all probability, attempted to exe-
cute her threats, for a scuffle ensued, in which the
candle was put out. The gaoler's wife, who had got

up naked to seek her husband, being sure that her vengeance would fall either on her faithless spouse, or on her rival, continued to lay about her manfully in the dark, and scratched and kicked Desire most ruefully, roaring out constantly, '*O the nasty hussey! O the good for nothing rogue!*'

Though I had some reason to complain of Desire, I was not sorry to have an opportunity of returning the good office she had done me a few days before, so *poking* my way through the hole in the wall, I hasted to her assistance. As my object was to separate the two female combatants, I was obliged, however painful it was to my modesty, to ascertain their sex. The gaoler's wife, either tired or satisfied with her revenge, took the same method to find out her husband, and not knowing that there was another man in the apartment, mistook me for him.

'Come along with me, you good for nothing fellow,' said she, still keeping her hold, and drawing me towards the door. I suffered her to lead me along; she turned the key on Desire and her husband, and we went downstairs in the same manner to her room, where a light convinced her of her mistake . . . .
. . . . *Hiatus* . . . .
. . . .

'Oh!' said the gaoler's wife, sighing, 'how sweet is revenge! but we have been here an hour, and I must go and separate that nasty hussey and my good for nothing husband. Only think, Mr. Corncob, what a misfortune for an honest woman to be married to such a nasty fellow.'

We found Desire and the gaoler both dressed, in expectation of the visit of this poor injured woman, who began anew to scold her husband, calling him a hundred times over a nasty fellow. However, as soon as the gaoler found an opportunity of interrupting her, 'Madam,' said he, 'you are pleased to be very severe on me, but I should be glad to know what you have been doing for this hour past with Mr. Corncob.'

'What I have been doing, you good for nothing wretch!' said the gaoler's wife, crying. 'Mr. Corncob knows that I was so affected at seeing I had brought another man into my chamber, that I fell into fits, from which I am but just recovered. Is it not true, Mr. Corncob?'

'Fits!' said I, 'I can safely say, madam, that I never saw stronger convulsions in my life.' As a man must have been an infidel indeed not to have been satisfied with the testimony of his own wife, the gaoler begged his spouse's pardon. She, poor woman, consented to be appeased, and the gaoler, the gaoler's wife, my dear Desire, and myself passed the rest of the night, if not more pleasantly, at least more quietly than we had done the preceding part.

Chapter 18

*Jonathan embarks on board a cartel-
ship bound to New-York.—The gallant
behaviour of Captain Quid, in the
battle—he would have fought with the
Picaroon, but for untoward
circumstances.—Proceedings of a
naval court-martial.*

M Y DELIVERY from prison, and my embarka-
tion on board an armed transport, which was
arrived as a cartel-ship from New-York, and was
destined to carry the prisoners at Boston to that
place, were attended by no remarkable circumstance, and I beg the reader will consider me as at
sea in a gale of wind, or, as most historians call it,
a storm or tempest. As I do not write by the sheet,
I will not employ half a dozen pages in a description of it, for a tempest has been so often described,
that it is now very generally understood, that in a
tempest the wind blows hard; that the wind occasions the sea to rise; that the sea tosses the vessel
about; that the motion of the vessel makes many
people sea-sick, and that those who are sea-sick
spew. I came upon deck for that purpose, and

pleased at finding my stomach somewhat easier, and inattentive to the noisy operations of the sea-men, was walking whistling up and down the quarter-deck, when three sailors took me up in their arms, and were going to throw me over-board.

'For G–d's sake, gentlemen,' said I, 'you would not in such cold blowing weather throw a man over-board so subject to the rheumatism as I am. It is not a fortnight since I had a touch of it in my shoulder.'

'D––n–tion to you,' said one of them, 'you lub-berly rascal, why are you whistling for wind then, when we cannot show a rag to the gale? does not it blow hard enough without your giving us your d––––d cheek musick, to bring on a squall, and be d––––d to you?'

I gave them my word that I never would whistle again when the wind blew, but, that to make them amends, I would whistle myself out of breath whenever they might happen to be in want of wind in a calm.—'Ah! d–mme,' said one of them, 'that's sensible talking.' And on this condition they con-sented not to throw me over-board.

The wind increased, a fog came on, we lost our foremast and bowsprit, and the captain of the transport, obliged to abandon the conducting of his vessel to the elements, was passing the night over a bottle of brandy, in company with Captain Quid, who was giving him an account of the gal-lant battle he would have fought with the *Picaroon* privateer, but for the difference in the weight of metal and the roughness of the sea.

'I would have laid him athwart hause,' said he,

'and raked him fore and aft till he had p–ssed himself—Oh! you may take my word for it, I would have done his business for him tightly, for from a boy, I never knew what it was to be afraid, and at ten years old I used to beat my three sisters, who were all older than myself—For sweet J–sus' sake, what is the matter upon deck?'

'The mizzen-mast is gone by the board.'

Captain Quid's teeth began to chatter.—'O Lord,' said he, 'I believe I have caught an ague in this blowing weather—pray give us another bottle of brandy; we have drunk but three between two.'

'The mizzen-mast is nothing,' said the captain of the transport; 'my little *Nancy* is as light as a cork, and her bottom is as tight as a bottle.'

'I am glad to hear it,' said Captain Quid; 'so, as I was telling you, after raking him fore and aft, I would have stuck my pistols and cutlass in my belt, and boarded him, and, if the rebels had not taken off their hats to the captain of a man of war, I would not have left one of their heads upon their shoulders, for I assure you I am a very pretty player of the back-stick—In the name of G–d, what is all that noise?'

'The main-mast is gone over the side,' said a voice upon deck.

'O dear! O L––d! O dear!' said Captain Quid, beginning to cry, 'I have got my old complaint the gripes; O dear! O dear! I never had such gripes in my life—ouh! ouh! where is your close-stool?—ouh! ouh! a-a-a-h, it is too late—'

I thought it high time to leave Captain Quid and go to bed, though I had little hope of being able to sleep. However, the rolling of the vessel, which

for a long time kept slumber at a distance, had at
length a contrary effect, the fatigue it occasioned
laying me in the arms of the kind god Morpheus.
How long I had enjoyed the blessing of sleep I
know not, when a violent shock put an end to my
tranquility. I started up, rubbed my eyes, and
when I was well awake, smelling somebody by my
bedside, I asked what was the matter.

'O dear! O L――d!' said Captain Quid, 'the ship's
aground.'

'So much the better,' answered I; 'I can assure
you I was tired of being at sea.'

'But,' said he, sobbing, 'we are on St. George's
Bank, and O dear! O dear! the ship will certainly
go to pieces. I wish I had been killed when the
Picaroon took us, for I am not afraid of any death
but drowning.—O dear! O dear! get up and pray,
Mr. Corncob, for G–d's sake.'

As I began to think the danger serious, I got up
and followed him to the captain's cabin, where, as
well as in every other part of the ship, everybody
was at prayers. For my part, I took up the litany,
at the place where I had left off in the crutch business at the prison. Captain Quid, sobbing between
every word, knelt down by my side, and repeated
part of the marriage ceremony; while the captain's
clerk, who had been accustomed to perform the
office of chaplain at sea funerals, recited all he
knew of the service for the burial of the dead. But
nobody prayed so loud as a common sailor, who,
during the whole night, roared out with great
fervency, 'L――d have mercy upon us! Ch――st have
mercy upon us!'

At the dawn of day, another sailor came running

down from deck, and addressing this pious Christian, asked him whether he would lend a hand to break open the spirit-room. The only answer he obtained was, Christ have mercy upon us, Lord have mercy upon us.

'Why, d––n your e––s, you snivelling fool,' said the other, we are not on St. George's Bank; the land is so near that you might heave a biscuit on shore.

'Is it, by G––?' said he that was praying: 'if that's the case, Jack, I'll lend you a hand, with all my heart. A drop of brandy will do me a great deal of good, for this d––n'd praying has made my throat as dry as a chasing-mat.'

The news the sailor had brought proved true. We were aground at no very considerable distance from Rhode Island. The wind diminished gradually till it became possible to venture ashore in the boats. However, while rowing to land, we were not only in danger of perishing from the roughness of the sea, but from the unquiet disposition of Captain Quid, who as often as he saw a large wave coming on one side of the boat, jumped over to the other, pretending that he was afraid of the salt water's spoiling his uniform coat. We at last prevailed on him to shut his eyes, and all got safe to the beach, except twenty-two sailors, who were of the party that broke open the spirit-room, and who, being too *tipsy* to get out of the ship, were drowned when she went to pieces a few hours after.

The Americans taking our situation into consideration, determined at first to consider us as prisoners, and to insist on our being exchanged a second time; but as Charles-Town had been lately taken, and a great number of their men were in the hands of the British troops, they thought it was the best policy on this occasion to behave with justice, and to send us round to New-York. As soon as we arrived, an order was given to try our captain and the ship's company by a court-martial, for the loss of the ship. We repaired, in consequence, on board a fifty-gun ship, where the court was assembled. Captain Quid finding himself taken into custody by the master at arms, who had a great naked cutlass in his hand, had an attack of the gripes, which delayed the trial for some time. However, about half a bottle of brandy having put his stomach to rights our lieutenant and master were called and examined. They severally deposed that the *Picaroon* outsailed our ship, and was of superior force, and said, that they thought they acted *prudently* in striking.

The gunner was then asked, whether the captain had neglected anything to save the ship. 'Gentlemen,' said he, 'I can safely say that the captain did all he could to get away, for I never saw a man brisker in making sail; but I do not know that there was any necessity for striking.'

'How so?' said the captain of the fifty-gun ship; 'did not the *Picaroon* outsail you?'

'Yes, to be sure, Sir,' answered the gunner.

'And pray,' rejoined the captain, 'was not the *Picaroon* of superior force?'

'She carried sixteen guns,' answered the gunner.

'And we had only fourteen, gentlemen,' said Captain Quid.

[113]

'Pray, gunner,' continued the member of the court-martial, 'did not the sea run so high that your firing would have been of very little use?'

'It is true,' said the gunner, 'that we should have had little chance of hitting the *Picaroon;* but as I do not suppose the *Picaroon* would have found it easier to hit us, in my opinion, there was no occasion for striking.'

'Hold your tongue, sirrah!' cried half a dozen captains together; 'how dare you to give your opinion? do you think seven captains of the navy have occasion for your opinion? You are only desired to say whether the captain neglected any thing to save the ship?'

'Gentlemen,' answered the gunner, 'all I can say is, that Captain Quid made sail like a lamp-lighter.'

The president having ordered the master at arms to take the gunner into custody, asked me if I thought the captain did right in striking. 'Certainly, Sir,' said I, 'for I was once in a privateer, the captain of which, being foolish enough not to strike when he was desired, had his head taken off, an hour and a half after, by a nine-pound shot.'

The president then observed to the court, that it was impossible in his opinion for Captain Quid to do otherwise than he had done. 'You know, gentlemen,' said he, 'that there is an article which positively forbids a wasteful expence of the king's stores and provisions. Now, gentlemen, as the ship rolled so deep, if Captain Quid had fired at the *Picaroon,* he would evidently have wasted powder and shot, and would have been liable to have been broke by a court-martial. It therefore appears to me impossible to censure him for doing otherwise.' He then ordered the court to be cleared: the opinions were taken, and the audience was again called in, when the president declared that Captain Quid was acquitted, and that the gunner was sentenced to be confined for three months, and to be suspended from pay and duty during that term, as a punishment for his disrespect to the court. Captain Quid burst into tears.

'Thank'e, gentlemen, thank'e,' said he, 'I knew I had nothing to fear from gentlemen like you, and *brother officers.*'

Chapter 19

In which it is proved, to the satisfaction of the most captious, that the most advantageous kind of study is novel reading.

SOME of my readers, whom the hope of information has led to accompany me thus far in
my *strange, eventful* history, doubting the authen-
ticity of my adventures, may perhaps consider their
time as ill-spent; but I caution them against deter-
mining hastily, as to the truth or fiction of the
occurrences I relate. At the first blush, the speaking of Aesop's asses, and of the steed of Balaam,
staggered my faith; but when I began to look about
the world with eyes of observation, I saw many
living instances that justified the grave historians
in whom these facts are found. Let me then advise
thee, O scrupulous reader, to remember the often-
cited words of the poet, *ridentem dicere verum
quid vetat?** and to believe that there is no style

*The often-cited words appear in Horace's first Satire, lines
24-25. 'Yet may not Truth in laughing Guise be drest?'
Philip Francis translated them in 1743.

in which truth may not be conveyed; nor any
language, however doctoral, that may not be the
vehicle of error. I appeal to thyself. Hast thou
never studied a learned author, who, treating of
the sciences, vaunts in the first page, his strict attention to truth, and the infallibility of his observations? or some sage historian, who declares in his
preface, that his only guide shall be impartiality?
or some dogmatizing theologian, who knows as
well the intentions and dispensations of the Divin-
ity, as if he wrote in the council chamber of the
seventh heaven? If so, I am full sure thou wilt confess, that thou hast sometimes, by intense coction
of ideas, muddled thy poor weak head to compre-
hend hard words, and to store thy mental magazine
with systems, facts, and articles of faith, which thou
hast deemed indisputable truths, no longer than
till thou hast met with some other authors, who,
discussing the same subjects, have proved to thee,
by argumentation equally painful, that thy revered
oracles were inspired by lying gods. I have not been
less unlucky. Towards the end of the last war,
tired of seeing in the English papers accounts of
victories obtained by Sir Edward Hughes, over the
Bailli de Suffrein, and in the French gazettes rela-
tions of battles, in which, at the self-same time, the
Bailli de Suffrein had beat Sir Edward Hughes, I
resolved to confine my reading to books not likely
to mislead me, and very properly determined to
begin with the Evangelists. Lieutenant Dasher, of
whom honourable mention has been made in this
work, was companion of my studies. In Matthew
and Mark we met with some passages, which, not

according exactly, were stumbling-blocks to our weak reason; but by our faith and piety we reconciled these little differences in the best way we were able. I read on, and towards the conclusion of Luke, found that this Evangelist counted two young men dressed in white, in the holy sepulchre, though St. Mark had said there was only one.

I paused and laid down the book, which was immediately shut by Lieutenant Dasher, who desired me to read no farther; for, said he, if you proceed we shall have a dozen of these *buckram angels*. I rebuked him duly for the indecency of the expression, but resolved to have recourse to the learned commentators of different sects, for the explanation of the obscurities of the text. Ah! well-a-day! how was I surprised to find the same words of the Gospel adduced by grave Roman Catholic priests, to prove that all Protestants would be broiled everlastingly, and brought forward by grave Protestant divines, to prove that the Roman Catholics would be roasted in eternal fire.

I then turned my attention to the sciences, and studied Newton, with whose account of the motion of the heavenly bodies I was perfectly well satisfied, and considered what he taught, not as a system, but as demonstrated truths, which were no longer held in doubt by any one. But alas! I was advised by a friend to read the first of all French philosophers, whose name is Jacques Henri Bernardin de St. Pierre, and who assured me that the system of Newton was no better founded than that of Descartes. What! the earth revolve round the sun! cries Jacques Henri Bernardin de St. Pierre. He swears by his gods it is vastly odd—he can never believe it. How is it possible, says he, that the fixed stars, which are no bigger than pins' heads, as we see them in the summer, should be still in sight in the winter, when, according to Newton, we are 160 millions of miles farther from them?

Bidding adieu to astronomy, which I considered as a science above the reach of human intelligence, I turned to that part of Newton which treats of light and heat; but, mercy on me! Jacques Henri Bernardin de St. Pierre came across my way again. I had been firmly convinced, by Newton's experiments, that light and heat were reflected from white bodies, and absorbed by others in proportion to the intenseness of the tint; till the learned Frenchman proved to me that Providence had made the birds white in cold countries, that they might derive greater warmth from the oblique rays of the sun, and of dark colours within the tropics, that they might be less exposed to the action of vertical heat. Surely, said I, in things which we may behold with undazzled eyes, and which may be questioned by the touch, the truth must be more perspicuous. In this persuasion, I directed my attention to natural history, and was highly pleased with Doctor Mead's account of the action of poisons: nothing appeared to me more evidently proved than the coagulation of the blood, by an acid salt in the venom of the viper; when, woe is me! the work of the Abbe Fontana falling into my hands, I there found a clear demonstration that Mead did not know what he was saying.—I heartily cursed all system makers; but at least, said

I, in matters of fact that have had thousands for witnesses, there can be no danger of deception; and so I began to read history. Every Englishman must be sensible, that being a descendant of Englishmen, my face glowed, and my pulse beat high when I perused the high deeds of arms of our sturdy forefathers. The Black Prince was not prouder of the battle of Crecy than I was. Every time I thought of the valorous actions of our ancestors there, I couched my oaken sapling, and should have done so to this day, if my curst fortune had not made me acquainted with a Flemish historian, in whom I found a long detail of the victory obtained by the Flanderkins over the French at Crecy in 1346, at which the author observes, as a trifling circumstance, that the King of England and some troops of his nation were present. Disappointed everywhere in my search of truth, I determined to give it up, and have since read nothing but novels. As in works of this kind, I expect only fiction, whenever I meet with a just observation, or a character drawn after nature, I consider it as clear gain. I advise my reader to follow my example, and assure him, that in that part of the adventures of Jonathan Corncob he has already perused, as well as in the sequel I may hereafter offer to the public, there is more truth, than is sometimes to be found in books with more promising titles.

FINIS

THE ADVENTURES OF
JONATHAN CORNCOB
has been set in Linotype Baskerville with dis-
play type in Foundry Cloister Black by Dix
Typesetting Company. It has been printed on
Simpson Lee Recycled Text and bound by
Murray Printing. The typographic design is
by John Anderson and the illustrations are by
Mark Livingston, who, acutely afflicted by
modesty and a refined sense of probity, has
provided the following credit.

*Of Hogarth's noble brother artist, Christopher
Wren, we are told on his tomb in St. Paul's what
is perfectly plain: 'Whoso would seek his monu-
ment, look round you.' So, let me anticipate the
querulous outcry of pundits and the quizzical
squint of the rest by announcing,—nay invok-
ing,—at once and with gusto, my Complete debt
to the inexhaustible Hogarth; and to the world
which, in its every fit, start, form, and nuance,
he has re-created in microcosm for all time. If I
cannot claim to have used his genius as skillfully
as it deserves, I will not have it said that I used
him skulkingly or ungratefully or, in the least
line, otherwise than with Reverence.*

—MCL